THE WINTER TRAVELERS

Also By Don J. Snyder

Veterans Park
A Soldier's Disgrace
From The Point
The Cliff Walk
Of Time & Memory
Night Crossing
Fallen Angel
Winter Dreams

THE
WINTER
TRAVELERS
A Christmas Fable

Don J. Snyder

Cover painting © Edward Spaulding DeVoe

Design by Lynda Chilton

ISBN 978-0-89272-922-7

Printed in the United States

5 4 3 2 1

BOOKS·MAGAZINE·ONLINE
www.downeast.com

Distributed to the trade by National Book Network

Library of Congress Cataloging-in-Publication Data

Snyder, Don J.

  The winter travelers / by Don J. Snyder.

      p. cm.

  ISBN 978-0-89272-922-7 (hardcover : alk. paper)

  1. Self-realization—Fiction. 2. Winter—Fiction. 3. Psychological fiction. I. Title.

  PS3569.N86W57 2011

  813'.54--dc23

                              2011027540

Once more for Colleen,
who always understood

And in memory of my father,
Richard, who was a soldier
on a train a long time ago.

I was a small boy in the 1950s, and my grandmother often walked me through our little town and showed me the houses where soldiers had lived until the day they left their parents for the Second World War, many of them taller than their fathers by then, but still young enough for the town to recall them as their mother's little boys. They left mostly modest walk-up row houses, joined at the shoulders, with windows facing the street. And in those days of the war, mothers hung small flags in the windows with a blue star for each son who was serving. When one of those sons died, a gold star was sewn over the blue one, and my grandmother would walk in her flower print dress to the mother's house with a casserole or pie and sit and talk with her, mostly just listening. And as she listened, she began to dream about the boys who had left this little town, never believing they might not return, and of the boys who made it back home to father a vast new generation of babies, with a look in their eyes like they wanted to get started in the next five minutes. Those soldiers, the lucky ones, came home and married their sweethearts and started having babies as fast as they could, and my grandmother believed that each time one of those babies was born, the soul that inhabited it came from one of the dead soldiers, so that those boys who had died so far from home got to live again in the town where they had grown up, the town they had left for the war. And all their lives, these children of the next generation, inhabited by the souls of the dead soldiers, would run through the quiet tree-lined streets playing, and later park their cars outside the movie theater, with the strange sense of familiarity, the sense that they had been there before and that all of this was happening to them once again.

BOOK I

ONE

*I*t had been a hard year in New York City for beggars and for princes. But with Christmas coming on once more, the search for meaning began again along the gaudy boulevards of commerce and down the unmarked alleyways of love, where all we know is what we remember, and where we still wait for someone who might cast a light over the walls of our hearts.

There was snow late that afternoon, big fat flakes swirling like scraps of paper through the slanting light in Manhattan, and as dusk neared, a cold mist rose up from the East River. You could feel it along the sidewalks among the shoppers hurrying home with their brightly wrapped packages. I don't mean the mist, I mean the emptiness, which we should call by its real name. Fear.

By then we were all afraid of something. Losing our jobs, or our money, or disappointing the people who depended on us, or being no longer blessed. I suppose we were afraid of being cut loose from what had protected us for so long and ending up as haunted, weary travelers on a night journey, bound for where we would never be certain again.

None of this was on the mind of the homeless woman sitting inside a cardboard box house above the steam grate on Park Avenue as night began to fall. This woman's house was ingeniously constructed of three washing machine boxes fitted inside each other like Russian dolls. It's easy to walk past these people, because we have seen so many of them in cities across America, refugees from some other life, stuffing newspaper inside their sleeves and shoes for insulation against the cold. In the town where I was a boy, my grandmother called them hobos, and she knew one of them by name. He was a man who had once lived a celebrated life in a mansion outside Philadelphia, where he had a room filled with telescopes and a miniature baseball field in his back yard, an exact replica of Ebbets Field in Brooklyn, where the Dodgers played, before he lost everything in the Great Depression and took up permanent residence in a rusting Georgia Pacific boxcar abandoned on the bank of the Schuylkill River.

This homeless beggar in her late twenties went by the name Cooper, rather than her full name, Sally Cooper, and she passed for a man beneath the rags and the dirt and the wool cap pulled down low. You would have had to look closely to notice her startling green eyes and the refined cut of her cheekbones in a face turned blue from the cold, as she stared with a depthless sorrow at the lighted Christmas tree in front of the big department store.

The holidays are tough on those in pain.

And they were on those in investment banking as well, that year.

Wall Street looked deserted that night. A few fat pigeons and one three-legged dog chasing the paper trash that moved along Stone and Hanover Streets in the wind. In the fading light, the neoclassical façade of The Exchange looked like an abandoned movie set. Some wise guy had tied a black plastic trash bag over the head of the charging bronze bull.

This did not sit well with the boss, who stood at the ornate, trimmed windows in the fifth-story offices of The Company, looking down into the street. He was a sixty-year old man, elegantly dressed in pin stripes and yellow suspenders, and when he had seen enough outside, he turned back to face a room filled with handsome young patricians sitting behind computer terminals, all of them looking like they were awaiting their execution. The room itself was adorned with gleaming, triple-crown molding, a gilded chandelier, and Persian carpets that Joseph P. Kennedy had purchased when he first occupied the space in 1938. One of the young men in the room, Charlie Andrews, a handsome thirty-year-old in a suit made of steel, had his head bowed almost to his knees and was breathing like he was going to have a heart attack.

"Turn off your damned machines," the boss cried out. And they followed his orders. One at a time the computer screens went black. His eyes moved slowly across the room before he spoke again. "You boys managed to do what two world wars and the bloody Great Depression couldn't do. You destroyed this magnificent company, and when I stand here looking at you now, do you know what I see? I see pigs at a trough. Pigs at a trough. Get out of my sight."

Slowly the handsome young princes rose to their feet and left the room. Charlie was the last to leave and he walked out by himself, a look of death across his face.

Against the approaching darkness, Cooper lit a wooden kitchen match, its bright spark transforming her cardboard house into a glowing box of light. Illuminated on one wall were two photographs cut from old *Life* magazines, like the ones my grandmother had often shown me when she spoke about the war. One was a giant troop ship, her decks crammed with soldiers waving as the boat slipped past the Statue of Liberty to begin her crossing to England. Another was the iconic picture of the sailor kissing the young woman in Times Square, bending her over in his embrace as a blizzard of ticker tape blew through Manhattan. A shadow history of America. And with these magazine photographs there was one personal black and white picture of a beautiful little girl, maybe six years old, in an elegant white dress, standing before a tall mirror in an exquisite frame of carved rose petals. There were no other people in the picture, just store mannequins in wedding dresses. The way Cooper gazed at the child, it must have been someone she lost. Maybe herself. There was a deep longing in her eyes as she studied the picture, the kind of longing that comes with a realization that when we lose the people we love best in this life, most of the time it is our own fault.

Just before her match went out, Cooper took the photograph from the wall, slipped it into her pocket, and made her way out into the night.

On the other side of the world, less than a mile away, was the Waldorf Hotel, lit up like a castle in Switzerland. Charlie Andrews had just checked in at the front desk. If he had not been wearing a three-thousand-dollar suit and four-hundred-dollar shoes, he might have aroused suspicion arriving for the night with no luggage, but as it was, he walked purposely to the bronze elevator doors and rose as weightless as a moth to the twenty-second floor. On the door knob, he hooked the little sign that said in four languages he did not want to be disturbed, opened a small bottle of Jack Daniels from the mini bar, poured it into a cut-crystal glass, and took his cell phone from his jacket pocket, glancing down at the lit screen that always comforted him in some way he had never tried to understand.

When he finished his drink, he drew back the shades, slid open the window, and looked down at the street. Directly below were two bellhops, dressed for a more dignified century in baroque capes and top hats. They were sneaking a cigarette, blowing plumes of smoke toward the sky where Charlie counted seven bright stars, pierced with light.

Cooper had reached a small boutique on Fifty-Seventh Street and stood at the glass windows looking at a display of beautiful dresses, an assortment of wedding gowns, and the loveliest little dress for a flower girl the world has ever seen.

A moment passed and then she turned up the collar of her ratty coat and bravely entered the store, which smelled like daffodils. A gust of cold wind swept into the shop from the street and before she could close the door, a bristling young woman in clicking heels approached from a back room, already calling out, "You'll have to leave."

Cooper tried to placate her with a smile. "I'll only be a minute," she said sweetly. "I was just hoping you'd found the dress."

"There's no dress here for you. I've already told you that. Now, you'll have to leave my store."

Cooper tried again, gesturing to the flower girl dress in the window as she said, "It looks just like that one."

"It doesn't matter to me what it looks like," the woman replied as she swung open the door. "Please don't come back here again, or I'll have to call the police."

She waited until Cooper had stepped outside, then locked the door and watched Cooper walk away.

In room 2217 at the Waldorf, his suit jacket off and the tails of his Ascot Changs shirt hanging out, Charlie sat in the Queen Anne chair before the open window, where he had lined up six empty bottles of Jack Daniels like toy soldiers. He was methodically deleting all the names and telephone numbers in his phone, one at a time. Each time he hit the delete button and another name disappeared, he recalled a girl he dated for a while, who told him that she would be happy to marry him just for the chance to watch him dress for work each morning. Trying to picture her face, he glanced toward the window and realized how remarkably still the world seemed. And with this stillness there was a cold bleakness somewhere in his chest, and a depression in his heart that had weight to it. And a quiet, bright darkness that took all the strength from him.

Cooper was back on the sidewalk watching people line up on the corner at a bus stop. The first in line was a black nurse or hospital technician of some kind, eating a slice of pizza. Behind her was a construction worker, his hard hat cocked rakishly to one side of his head, which was covered in a red bandana. And the last in line was an elderly man with thick white hair, as white as the snow falling from above him. He stood with a cane in his right hand.

Finally the bus approached and came to a stop. The first two people entered the bus and as the elderly man reached the first step, Cooper saw something fall from his pocket into the snow. While she waited for the bus to pull away, she decided to keep whatever the man had lost.

If it had been a wallet, she would have kept the money and given the rest to the first policeman she saw. She had done that before. She had once overheard someone say that in this city of eight million people, more than seven hundred lose their wallets every single day. According to the police, the number had risen sharply once people began having more things to keep track of. iPods. Cell phones. Tiny digital cameras.

Tonight what Cooper found in the snow was a cell phone, worth five dollars at the pawn shop, and as she walked there she had the luxury of deciding whether she would eat something tonight, or save the money for breakfast in the morning.

There was a line of refugees inside the pawnshop, each of them asking the Korean man behind the counter for more than he was offering, before grimly settling for his price. The man in front of Cooper had a gash across the back of his neck that looked like it had been stitched up on a sewing machine. She was counting the stitches when the phone began ringing in her hand. The sound, an old swing tune with a loud bass drum, startled her, and after a moment when she couldn't figure out how to silence it, the owner of the pawnshop yelled at her. "Hey, Einstein! Take that noise outside!"

Out on the sidewalk, she walked in a circle with the sound of a band playing in the palm of her hand. It seemed to be playing louder now and no matter how many of the lighted buttons she pushed, it wouldn't stop, until suddenly there was a man's voice speaking to her with these words, "It's Charlie. I've lost all your money. Everything you ever said about me was true. I'm going to make it easier for both of us, Pop. I'm going to kill myself tonight."

The words took her breath away. She felt her knees tremble and she stumbled across the sidewalk and leaned against a building as the voice said, "Are you there?"

She glanced quickly at the world around her, looking for an answer. She saw a couple walk past her, arm in arm. She saw the white snow mounting softly on a window ledge. And bright stars above her, which began to drift across the dark sky as she grew dizzy, and she lay her face against the granite building and closed her eyes. When she opened them again, she was staring at an ornate carved angel that looked straight into her eyes.

"Your father wants to talk to you," she said into the phone. "Where are you, Charlie?"

And then she began running through the snow as she held the phone to her ear. At an intersection, she stopped and took a second to get her bearings, then turned left and ran through the traffic as cars and buses honked their horns at her. Soon she was running right up the center of Park Avenue, weaving her way between moving cars, some whose drivers rolled down their windows and cursed at her, others who, despite the fact that they had grown familiar with the city's sad parade of troubled souls, locked their doors until the crazy woman in rags had passed.

By the time she reached the Waldorf, it was snowing harder and a small crowd of people had gathered on the sidewalk, some were pointing up at the open window where a man stood in its frame, his shirttails blowing in the wind. Cooper moved through them until she came face to face with one of the bellhops and said the first thing that came into her mind. "I know him. Get me up there."

TWO

*I*n the elevator, Cooper looked down at the stains on her pants while she spoke to Charlie. "I just want to give you your father's phone," she said, "and then I'll leave. I'm in the elevator now." Rising through the air with her were the manager, whose bald head gleamed under the ceiling light, a maintenance man carrying a steel ring of keys, and an elderly woman with a small white dog on a rhinestone-studded leash. They stood as far away from Cooper as the small space would allow, and when the elderly woman stepped off on the thirteenth floor she looked back at Cooper before the doors slid closed and said, "This is the Waldorf, you must have made a wrong turn somewhere."

Cooper bowed her head. She had a sense of her own terrible fragility, her bones turning brittle as hollow glass this winter.

The maintenance man unlocked the door to Charlie's room and she stepped in behind him and the manager. From the threshold she could see Charlie standing in the open window, holding his cell phone to his ear.

"I'm here now," she said into the phone and when he turned to face her and their eyes met for the first time, a quiet calm spread through her, and she walked purposefully past the other two men, crossing the room so that she was close enough to speak to Charlie without raising her voice. By now the wind was blowing harder and the white curtains enveloped him like wings. He had turned away from her but when she called to him, he turned back slightly and regarded her. He looked confused and frightened in his beautiful suit, which was fluttering in the wind.

Cooper smiled at him. "Your father dropped his phone in the street tonight," she said. "Lucky me, I found it."

Charlie's face went blank before he turned to the dark night and the street below, as if Cooper didn't exist. She took a step closer to try to draw him back. "Listen," she said. "Your father loves you, no matter what—"

He cut her off and said, "No matter what I've done?"

She thought for a moment, then said, "No matter what's happened to you."

When Charlie stretched his arms out at his sides, like he was going to try to fly from his perch, she said the next thing that came into her mind. "I grew up in a small town in Northern California. There's a lake there, and when it's really calm and still, the stars are reflected across the water like they're drowning."

This left her breathless as she waited. Finally Charlie looked at her and he seemed to be waiting for her to say something more, so she went on. "When I was a little girl my mother taught me to sail a small boat. It's still there. If you can get me there, Charlie, I'll sail with you through the stars. Would you like to do that?"

Their eyes met again and she said one more thing as she watched him looking at her, as if he was trying to decide why in the world he should believe this beggar in rags. "I've been trying to get back there. Have you ever really wanted to get somewhere, but there's a heaviness on you and you just can't move?" she asked him.

He didn't seem to hear. "My boss has a sailboat," he said.

"Oh," she said at once. "What kind?"

"A yacht," he replied. "Only by next week it will be repossessed. I lost all his money on Tuesday. I lost everybody's money."

He gazed out at the night sky as a pained look settled in his eyes. Then he asked, "How did you get my father's phone?"

"It fell from his pocket into the street," she answered.

He looked away, turning his head slowly. "Was he drunk?"

"I wouldn't know that," she said.

"He's been drinking ever since I was born. He worked his whole life for me at a paint factory in Hoboken. Most of it on the night shift. He put me through college and business school. When he retired, I persuaded him to take his pension in a lump sum and let me invest it. It was forty-two years of work. When things went bad last summer, I lost half of it. I tried to make it back in the commodities market. That's a tough climb. Do you know anything about the commodities market?"

Cooper answered right away. "No, I don't. I'm sorry, Charlie."

"Well," he said. "The price of corn is determined by fourteen unrelated factors, including the price of fertilizer and who's in power in Moscow. I lost it all."

"We lose things, Charlie. That's life. At least he's still got you."

"He's been telling me for ten years that I lost my moral compass. Those are his words for a playboy."

"What about your mom?" she asked.

"She died five years ago. I promised her that I would take care of him," he said.

This thought seemed to weigh on Charlie. Suddenly he leaned toward the open air, like he was ready to jump now, like he had been stalling Cooper rather than the other way around.

"Can I tell you something, Charlie?" she said. And then she waited for him to turn his face to her. "Most of us miss the real story."

"What real story?" he asked.

"The story we were put in this world to live."

"Why do we miss it?"

"Because it's not about us, it's about someone else. We're only a part of it."

They looked at each other for a length of time, which was magnified by the silence.

"I want to give you something, Charlie," Cooper said, and she watched him pull back slightly as she took off her necklace.

"What is it?" he asked.

"I'll just put it in your hand. Is that okay? It's a St. Christopher necklace."

Slowly, Charlie let go of the window frame and reached for her. She took hold of his hand. They were still looking at one another, motionless, as if they had just finished a dance, and then she pulled him gently inside, right into her arms. He looked awkward in her embrace, but only for an instant before he surrendered. Then he slumped down on the floor with relief.

"Were you lying about the stars?" he asked.

"I'm a coward," she said, "but I'm not a liar."

Next he asked her name. "Cooper," she said.

"My mom died from worrying," he said. "Every time Pop got in a car, she thought he would run someone over. But she never stopped loving him."

"That's love," Cooper said.

Charlie put out his hand for her to shake. She took it and shook it slowly. "It's nice to meet you," she told him. "Someone told me something once about alcoholics. The alcoholic can lie, cheat, and steal with the indifference and efficiency of a spider tearing the wings off a moth in its web. Lies are his currency. His compass. Place him inside a house of lies, and he will make his way from room to room without knocking into the furniture. He is such a thorough liar that he cannot be tricked by a lie. Only the truth can deceive him."

He thought about her words and said, "I guess that's my father."

"That's a lot of people," Cooper said. Then she remembered the maintenance man and manager. She turned and saw them standing as lifeless as statues. "You can leave us now," she said as she closed the window and locked it.

They started to walk to the door when Charlie called after them, "Do you suppose we could we get some room service?"

The manager looked back at him, hesitating for a moment in his surprise before he replied, "Certainly."

THREE

*B*ecause Charlie had grown up with a mother of Irish ancestry—the granddaughter of immigrants who fled County Wicklow during the great famine with nothing but the clothing on their backs and the shared belief that they could earn a place in eternity by opening their hearts to the lost and the dispossessed— he would not let Cooper go without feeding her first, and while they waited for their dinner to arrive, he insisted that she take a hot bath.

She stepped inside a room with a white marble floor, wainscoting painted the palest shade of green, and soft, glowing lights mounted to the walls beneath tulip-shaped glass shades. She closed the door behind her and locked it as she called to him, "If you live a good life, this must be the kind of bathroom they have for you in heaven."

She started the water running in the claw-footed tub.

"I ordered us the rack of lamb, is that all right?" He called back to her.

"Fine. Are you drinking the black coffee?"

"Yeah," he replied, "but I'd prefer a latte from Starbuck's."

"Sorry," she said. "These are tough times."

"You're telling me," he said.

"So, other than his drinking, is your father a good guy?"

"Yeah. He just never should have had a kid. He was old, twenty years older than my mom, and I guess as soon as I was born, he went off the deep end with the booze. Before she died, she asked me to forgive him and told me that something happened to him in the war, World War Two, before she was even born. She didn't know what it was; he'd never talked about it."

Cooper leaned close to the door. "I think you'd better take care of yourself, Charlie," she said, "in case your father needs you someday."

"Yeah, maybe," he said, as if he were thinking it over carefully.

While steam filled the room, she undressed in front of the full-length mirror, and the geometry of her body emerged improbably from the rags that concealed it. It had been a long time since she had seen her reflection, and the effect was disconcerting. Time, we know, is the great silent thief, busy every minute of every day, stealing our beauty and our strength. At first Cooper had the sense that she had caught the thief at work. She found she could only glance quickly and then look away. It was like reading only so far into a book and then returning it to the shelf to spare yourself the heartbreaking events that were about to unfold. The new lines around her eyes that she had never seen before were only the beginning. She was tempted to lean closer to examine them, but she thought better of this and took a seat in a wicker chair while she waited for the tub to fill. She looked down at the bruises on her legs and the swollen veins in her feet.

"How much money did you lose, Charlie?" she asked.

He answered right away as if he had been listening on the other side of the door, just waiting for her to ask him this. "All told, sixty-three million up in smoke," he said.

"You'll make it all back," she told him. "You guys always end up on top. It's just a big poker game."

"Monopoly, actually," he said.

She smiled at this. "So you were doing pretty well before the bottom fell out?"

"I made just under four million last year. Three the year before. Take-home cash, I mean."

"That's a lot of money, Charlie."

"It's all relative."

"Relative to what?"

"To what my bosses were pulling in."

"And I'll bet you guys all thought the mothers on welfare were getting fifty bucks a week too much."

"That's me," he said. "Sorry."

"It's never too late to be sorry," she said. "Did you save any of the millions you made?"

"Not a dime," he confessed.

The last thing she did before she sank into the hot bath was stand the photograph of the little girl in the beautiful white dress on the counter across from the tub so she could stare at it. As she slid into the water she called to him once more. "Charlie?"

"Yes?"

"Come to the door so you can hear me."

"Okay."

"Are you listening?"

"Yes, I can hear you."

"I want to be honest with you about something, Charlie. The only reason I came here to stop you from jumping is because I thought there might be something in it for me. I wasn't being brave. I don't have any bravery left in me. But when I was running up Park Avenue to get to you, I felt something coming back to me. Some of my dignity, I think. So, I want to thank you. Thank you for not jumping, Charlie, because I have to go home, and I wasn't going to be able to go without any dignity. But I think I'm ready now, if you'll help me."

The warmth of the bath was intoxicating, and she spoke to him for a long time, not realizing that he had fallen asleep on the floor on the other side of the closed bathroom door. Her voice, which had become calm and melodic, drifted through the room like light.

"My fiancé just got back from the war. His name is

Paul. He's a good man. You'd like him. I was working in an orphanage while he was gone. I'm supposed to pick up a dress for my flower girl in a bridal shop on Fifty-Seventh Street. But there's a little problem with money. I keep telling them that I have already paid for the dress, only they won't believe me, Charlie. Maybe if you were to come to the store with me?"

As she said this, she stepped into the room, wrapped in one of the luxurious Waldorf robes, holding the photograph in her hand and staring at it so that she almost tripped over Charlie.

She caught her balance and knelt down to study his sleeping face. The long eyelashes that looked brand new. The red blush of his cheeks. What she saw at once was the boy in his man's face, and she was drawn to him in exactly the opposite way she had been repelled by her own reflection in the bathroom mirror. She had the feeling that she had known him years ago and was now beginning to remember him. And this feeling drew her nearer to him until she could feel his breath on her face. She moved back just before she called his name softly to wake him. "Charlie?" When he didn't stir, she touched his shoulder and said his name again, and then when he first opened his eyes they were filled with such surprise and confusion that she felt like she had been caught trespassing. "I'm sorry," she told him quickly. "I should have let you sleep."

"No," he said, as he straightened his shoulders and leaned back against the door, staring at her. "It's just, well, look at you. I mean, you surprised me."

She felt herself blushing. "The bath was lovely," she said. "I think I used all the hot water."

His eyes widened and he smiled at her and told her that she looked beautiful. "I had no idea," he said.

"Well, anyway, here I am," she said. She lowered her eyes and when he saw that he had embarrassed her, he apologized.

She watched him put out his hand for her to shake. "Your name?" he said. "You didn't tell me your name."

"Cooper," she said as she shook his hand. "Sally Cooper."

"May I call you Sally?" he asked.

"That would be fine," she said. "But Charlie, I need you to help me. Will you help me?"

He didn't answer her at first. He just looked at her as if he were trying to memorize the features of her face. Then while he continued to stare, he told her that he would.

FOUR

*T*hey approached the little bridal shop on Fifty-Seventh Street just as the proprietor was hanging the CLOSED sign on the glass door. Charlie rushed into action, hurrying to the door ahead of Sally.

"What time do you close?" he asked the woman.

"Six," she said tersely.

Charlie looked at his watch. "It's only five till," he said.

"Trust me, we're closed," she said.

Charlie gave her the smile that had always made the girls at the company swoon. "Come on," he said. "Business can't be that good in this economy."

"Business is fine," she said with a little grin, and then looked past him and saw Sally standing on the sidewalk in the snow. Charlie took that moment to slip his foot between the door and the threshold.

"Look," she said, "you seem like a nice enough guy, I don't know who you are, but she's been here before. Every day for the last ten days, she's come here saying she has a dress to pick up for her flower girl."

This was deeply disturbing for Charlie, and he glanced back at Sally. The cold blue had returned to her face, and dressed again in her rags, she looked like any of the crazy people he had passed before in the city, vaguely taking note of them and then never giving them a second thought.

"Okay," he said to the woman. "I'm on a fool's errand here, you're right. But I owe her something. Have you let her inside your store before?"

She shook her head no.

"Will you just let us come in for a few minutes? Just to humor her? One act of kindness at Christmas, what do you say?" Charlie took out his wallet and opened it. He wanted her to see that it was stuffed with bills.

"Maybe I'll buy her a dress," he said.

"Our dresses come from Paris," she told him. "You'd need more money than that."

He looked into her eyes, smiled once more and said again, "One act of kindness, what do you say?"

She looked past him, then up at the night sky as she drew her bangs across her forehead. "Five minutes," she said, swinging open the door. "I don't know what kind of wedding she thinks she's going to, but I'm sure glad I wasn't invited."

"Yes," Charlie said, as he gestured for Sally to follow him inside. Then he leaned close to the woman and whispered to her. "You get that way when you work in this city for too long."

When she turned back and glared at him, he smiled

once more and said, "We won't take too much of your time. What's your name?"

"Gloria," she said.

"G L O R I A, like the old song," he sang for her. She said nothing, and Charlie watched as her eyes followed Sally across the room, which was lit with rouge colored paper lanterns that hung from the ceiling and dropped oblongs of light, like pink eggs, onto the mahogany floor. The dresses were displayed sumptuously on mannequins frozen in artful poses of staggering indifference. With their bald heads, they looked like chemotherapy princesses in fairy tales about cancer survivors. Sally walked among them like she was walking in her sleep, her arms out in front of her, turning first to one dress, and then another, as if the mannequins were whispering to her.

"Don't they look real, Charlie?" she called to him. She stepped close to one of them and stared into its bright, vacant eyes. Just as she raised her hand, the owner said, "No touching anything," and Sally let her arm fall, and bowed her head like a scolded child.

The woman retreated behind the counter, heels clicking with authority against the hard wood floor. Charlie followed her and stood next to the cash register, just across from her. "I'll have a double scotch, please," he said as a joke, but it got no reaction from her. "So," he said, "how much do you get for these dresses from Paris?"

"A lot," she answered.

He took out a business card almost as a reflex, but then he remembered that those days were gone, and he slid it back inside his pocket.

"Let me guess," she said abruptly. "You lost a lot of money and now you're hoping that if you do a little charity work, God or Fate will turn things around for you." She had that little grin again when she finished.

"You have a beautiful smile," Charlie said. This made her touch her face self-consciously and when she caught herself, she began to blush. "And you're absolutely right," he told her. "Right now I'm leaning pretty hard on God and Fate."

"I thought so," she said. "So, if you've lost all your money, how do you plan to pay for a dress for your friend? I won't take your credit cards."

"Whoa!" he said, theatrically. "You won't take plastic? What's the Republic coming to?"

"The Republic is coming to crap, thanks to you guys."

It was no longer funny to him. Just sad. "Do you believe that?" he asked her.

"I believe you ought to be ashamed of yourself," she told him.

He looked right into her eyes. "Guess what?" he said. "I am."

Their eyes met briefly and then she called to Sally again. "I told you not to touch anything."

Sally had placed her hand on a mannequin's arm. "I'm sorry," she said. "Right over here in the corner, you used to have a beautiful mirror."

Neither Charlie nor the woman was really listening. By now they were more interested in each other. "So where do you live?" Charlie asked her.

"Greenwich," she said. "In the winter."

"What about summer?"

"The Hamptons."

"That must be quite a commute."

"It's not bad. My brother owns a helicopter."

Charlie's eyes opened wide. Then he nodded his approval. "And when you close up here, do you ever go out for drinks?"

"I've been known to do that."

Music to Charlie's ears. "That's good, Gloria, because life is short. You want to make the most of it."

He was so adept at this dance that he could make you feel like you were leading the way. He had her eyes already swimming in his, when he pushed up the sleeve of his coat again and slipped off his watch. "Could I buy her a dress for fifty-two thousand? This is a Patek Phillipe from their Grand Complications Collection. There is a museum in Geneva on Rue Des Vieux Grenadiers with nothing in it but these watches. This one retails for fifty-two thousand, seven hundred, and forty dollars."

Without averting her eyes she asked, "How do I know it's not a knock off?"

Charlie held it out for her. "You're just going to have to trust me, I guess." He placed it in her hand and as she ran her fingers across the polished yellow gold, he could tell that she was interested.

Sally called to them again. "The dress had tiny, pale blue flowers embroidered on the wrists and collar. Here, let me show you."

She walked to the counter and stood beside Charlie as she showed them her photograph. She pointed to the lovely mirror. "That was the most beautiful mirror," she explained. "You can see the roses carved on the frame. It was standing over there in the corner."

It was the earnest way she believed this that made Charlie feel so sorry for her. Sorry enough that he was willing to try anything.

"Why don't you check your records, Gloria?" he asked with a sly wink. "You must have all your records right here in your computer." He looked at her until finally she played along with him.

"What's your name, ma'am?" she asked.

Sally turned and smiled at her. "No one has called me ma'am in a long time," she said. "I'm Sally. Sally Cooper." She thrust her hand out for the woman to shake, but she declined and stared at her computer screen as she typed in Sally's name. She scrolled down a long list, hesitated, and glanced at Charlie before she announced that she had found it. "Right here," she said flatly. "Here's your name. It looks like I owe you a dress for your flower girl."

"Well, that's wonderful isn't it, Sally?" Charlie exclaimed with a bit too much enthusiasm.

Sally looked deeply into his eyes and for a moment he thought she might have caught his trick. Then she turned to the owner. "I'm sorry it's taken me so long to come pick up the dress," she said. "When you're lost, time just seems to fade away."

FIVE

*C*harlie sat in a beautiful upholstered wing chair watching the owner wrap the dress in white tissue paper, as Sally looked on.

"Well, that should just about do it, then," she said and turned to him. "I'll put this in a box and you can be on your way."

As she walked past Charlie she whispered to him, "I'll take the watch now."

"Of course," Charlie said, slipping it into her hand. "I wonder though if you could do me one more favor." He had hold of her hand by the wrist. "I know I'm pressing my luck, but I was hoping you might let her try on one of your wedding dresses."

She scowled, and said, "How come I knew you were going to ask me that?"

He waited a moment before answering her. "I know it's a little crazy," he said.

"Crazy?" she said. "You must think I'm crazy."

"No, not at all, Gloria," he told her.

She glanced at Sally and then looked back at Charlie. There was no denying his charm and his handsome face.

He seemed to have a kind of personal velocity that swept people along and made him difficult to oppose. She felt her resolve weakening.

Charlie felt it, too. He knew that he possessed a certain power to get what he wanted in this world. In the past, before his work turned to ashes, he had always believed he was special, and that someone was watching over him. And now as he began to feel renewed, the dark time he had spent on the window ledge at the Waldorf was beginning to feel like the dumbest thing he had ever done in his life, which made him feel even more grateful to Sally.

"Are you going to tell me that I should let your friend try on a wedding dress, just to be kind?"

Charlie smiled at her again, then said, "It's a chance for you to cover your bets, just in case it turns out that there is such a thing as God. Or Fate."

He watched the owner closely as she chose a wedding gown for Sally to try on and showed her to the dressing room. When she returned, she knelt down to wipe dust off a glass display case of jewelry, while he weighed his chances and imagined the possibilities. And then Sally emerged from the changing room and it was like music had suddenly begun to play. One look at her and Charlie sensed that the lever of some gigantic engine had been thrown, and an iron wheel was set rolling on its rail. Is this love, we wonder? Infatuation? Or simply the power of physical beauty to surprise us? He felt the layers of the earth shift with a sudden understanding that all his life had been leading him to this moment. She looked regal in the long white gown with strands of miniature pearls sewn around the neck and wrists. And he couldn't move his eyes from her as she turned gracefully in the rose colored light.

"When is your wedding?" he heard himself ask, this question barely rising above the chorus inside his head that said, You can't ever marry anyone but me.

"Christmas day," she said, as she studied her profile in a mirror.

"Six days," Charlie said. "You don't have much time."

"No, not much time."

Then she looked into his eyes with great seriousness, "You believe me, don't you, Charlie?"

The shop owner witnessed the transformation in Charlie, and seeing how suddenly his attention had shifted from her to Sally, she felt something cold pass through her.

Charlie answered. "And, this fellow, Paul? Is his name Paul?"

"Yes," Sally replied.

"Paul is waiting for you, right?"

"He's in California. A little town named BoisVert. That's a French name; it means green woods. That's where the lake is that I told you about."

"What I meant is," Charlie said, "is he still waiting?"

Sally turned to him, surprised by the doubt in his question. "Why wouldn't he be?" she asked. "Wouldn't you wait for me, Charlie."

Charlie was spellbound. He could hardly get out the words. "Yes," he said. "Yes, I'd wait."

"How long would you wait?" she wanted to know now.

"I guess I'd wait a long time. For as long as it took."

Sally let some time pass so that his words could hang in the silence between them. "That's very reassuring. Thank you, Charlie."

They were out on the sidewalk hailing a taxi when Gloria slid the watch into the safe. What a long, strange day it had been, she thought. Every day the world, and in particular this city, seemed to grow more odd and difficult to comprehend.

She walked into the back room to get her coat. Above her, on the stamped tin walls dating back to when her grandfather first bought the store, were old photographs she had seen thousands of times across the years since she first began working here during her summers off from Mount Holyoke. She usually ignored them because they seemed to mock her in some way, reminding her that she swore she would never spend her life in this shop, the way her grandparents and then her parents had. Tonight one photograph caught her eye. She glanced at it from a distance and then stepped closer to it, close enough to confirm that the mirror in the picture was the same she had seen in the homeless woman's photograph. The mirror with its frame of carved roses. She felt the air rush from her lungs and heard the sound of her keys striking the floor as they fell from her hand.

SIX

*T*he wind had come up outside, and they bowed their heads against the blowing snow as they ran to the cab. Sally carried the flower girl dress in a lovely octagon shaped box. Charlie opened the door for her and they slid into the back seat.

"Where you going?" the driver barked. He had a handlebar moustache and looked at their reflection in his rearview mirror, from which a rosary and the day's lottery ticket hung.

"I'll get you to the airport and buy your ticket home," Charlie said to Sally. "That's the least that I can do."

"You have enough money?" she asked.

"I'm the last of the big spenders," Charlie said. "When it's gone I think I'm actually going to feel relieved. I've spent so much time worrying about it and counting it these past seven months."

"Where you going?" the driver asked again.

"We haven't decided yet," Charlie called to him. "Turn your meter on."

The driver shrugged and started the meter. Under his breath he said, "It's your dime, big shot."

Sally looked out the window at the falling snow. "Charlie, I don't like flying. I've only flown once, and it scared me half to death," she said.

"When was that?" he asked.

She bowed her head. "A while ago," she said. When she looked up, he was looking at her. Their eyes met, and she looked away. Then she looked back again.

"I think you got lost a long time ago," Charlie said. "So did I, to tell you the truth."

Sally nodded and asked him if he had ever been to California?

"Pebble Beach to play golf, that's all."

"It snows seven months of the year where I live in Northern California," she told him. Then she stopped suddenly, as if she had nothing more to say, and glanced out the window. She seemed to vanish into her own thoughts and memories, as Charlie concentrated hard on her face, slowly going over each thing she had told him since their lives coincided, turning over the scraps of information, trying to construct a coherent story with a line of logic that would explain to him why she had become a homeless woman on the streets of Manhattan. He had to admit that he didn't believe she had a home in California, or anywhere, and so he pushed the point. "Do you want to call home first?" he asked.

She was still turned away when she wiped the frost off the taxi window. "Have you seen pictures of this city right after the war? There were soldiers and sailors in Times Square. The war had just ended, and everyone was throwing confetti from the windows. It was like snow."

"You mean the pictures after World War Two?" Charlie asked.

"Yes. In those days soldiers came home by train. There were troop trains. Some of them were a mile long. That's how a soldier should return from a war, don't you think, Charlie? A long, slow train ride across the beautiful countryside, to anticipate, mile after mile, just how wonderful it will be to finally come home again. After so long. After so many years far away."

He watched her brush her hair back from her face as he thought about what she had said, the simple words painting a vivid picture across the walls of his mind, so that he could actually *see* this train filled with soldiers, just as he had *seen* the boat sailing through the stars when she described it to him as he stood on the window ledge at the hotel.

"Where is Paul returning from?" Charlie asked her. "The war in Iraq?"

"He's in the Special Forces," she said solemnly. "He's fought all over the world."

She stopped and for a moment it seemed like she had nothing more to say. But then she went on. "When they came home that slow way by train, they looked out the windows and told themselves they were trying to see how the country had changed since they'd been gone. But really, they were trying to see how they had changed. I've changed since I last saw Paul. I'm not sure he'll even recognize me."

"Of course he will," Charlie said reassuringly. And then he asked her one more question as a test of what she had told him. "How long did it take?"

She faced him with a puzzled look. "How long did what take?" she asked.

He could tell that she had no idea what he was asking her and decided to dismiss everything she had told him. "Nothing," he said with a pleasant smile.

"Where are you two going?" the cab driver asked again.

Charlie was looking into Sally's eyes when he answered, "Penn Station."

SEVEN

*I*nside the echoing, murmurous hall of the station, Sally stood alone on the polished marble floor, gazing up at the enormous computerized board showing trains arriving and departing, white digital lights blinking next to their track numbers. She was clutching the eight-sided box tightly and to all who passed, she appeared to be alone in the world. But the forlorn look disappeared as Charlie came toward her through the crowd of night travelers. "I bought your ticket," he said and as he took it from his pocket to show her, she gestured to the board.

"In the old days, Charlie, that was all done manually. There was a catwalk up there and three men in suspenders and visors put up the numbers like a scoreboard at a baseball game. I can show you a book in the library that tells all about it."

Charlie nodded, then told her that her train to Chicago left in an hour.

"Chicago. The windy city," she said.

"You'll have a three-hour and ten-minute layover, then you catch a train to the west coast at nine thirty tomorrow morning. You'll be in California in eighty-one hours."

"You're good with numbers," she told him.

"I used to think so."

"I'm feeling dizzy, Charlie," she said, as her knees quivered and she leaned against him. He put his arm around her and helped her to a bench, just as his cell phone began ringing. He glanced down at the number on the lighted screen. "It's my boss," he said. Looking scared to death, he slipped the phone into the pocket of his suit coat.

"You're not going to talk with him?" Sally asked.

Charlie took the phone from his pocket and played the message his boss had left. "You're not off the hook that easy, pal. Call me."

Hearing this made him feel even worse. He put the phone in his pocket again.

"Maybe you should call him," Sally said.

"I can't call him," Charlie told her.

"What are you going to do then? Did you really lose everyone's money?"

Charlie nodded grimly.

"Are you a good stock broker?" she asked. "Can you make the money back?"

"I was good. I was always a good salesman."

"What made you a good salesman?"

Charlie didn't have to think about this; he knew the answer. "What made me good was that I never really cared," he said. "I never cared about anything. Then about five months ago, after things started going bad, I'd get these calls from my clients who had lost half of their kids' education funds, or the money they had saved to take care of their parents in old age, or their own retirement accounts and they'd say, 'Is it going to be all right, Charlie? Am I going to recover from this?' That's when I started caring. I kept hearing their stories, you know? I'd stay up all night staring at my computer screen, trying to come up with some new plan. But everything I tried only made it worse. I cared too much."

Sally thought about this, then asked him, "How can you care too much, Charlie?"

He turned the question over in his mind. *How can you care too much?* Then his phone began ringing again. He took it from his pocket and stared down at it and couldn't answer. With each ring he slid down lower on the bench where they were sitting. As soon as the last ring stopped, a frightened, almost panicked expression swept over his face and he jumped to his feet. "I have to get out of here," he exclaimed. "Are you going to be okay?"

"Where are you going?" she asked.

"I don't know," he told her. "I really have no idea."

"Why don't you come with me?"

It took a second for him to realize what she was asking him to do.

"To California?" he said.

"To the mountains. And to the lake. It might be good for you. I'd like you to come to my wedding."

But now he no longer believed in this wedding. He took a deep breath and tried to remember the last time his life had felt right to him. "I can't," he said softly.

She smiled at him serenely. "I wanted you to meet Paul."

He was close to confronting her, demanding to know if she was making up the wedding and Paul, when she said, "Every man wants to be a woman's first love, and every woman wants to be his last."

"Who said that?" he asked.

"Paul," she told him. "He wrote it for me in a poem."

Charlie looked right into her eyes. "He's a poet?"

"Oh yes, he's always written poems for me."

He searched her face for a trace of doubt or some sign that she was wavering, but found only absolute conviction. "I'll tell you what, Sally," he said slowly. "There's this girl I know in Chicago. We were in business school together. She told me if things ever went really bad for me, she would run away with me."

"She must have been in love with you," Sally replied with a smile.

"No, she's smarter than that," Charlie said. "But I'm going to call her. If she says I can crash at her place for a while, then I'll ride the train with you as far as Chicago. How about that?"

With a demure look in her eye, Sally said, "Call her, Charlie."

Charlie dialed the number. It began to ring and when a voice came on, they both had the same hopeful look. But then it turned out to be only the voice of a recorded message. "I'm not here right now to take your call."

"Well," Charlie said, "I tried."

"Thank you for trying," Sally said. "You were testing Fate, weren't you?"

"I guess I was," he said,

"Do you believe in Fate?" she asked.

"I've always said that I didn't. I don't really know. Maybe now I believe more in things we can't prove than in things that are supposed to be a sure bet. Things like General Motors and General Electric."

Sally took his hand. "Your father has beautiful white hair," she said. "I was looking at his hair when he stepped onto the bus."

Charlie looked away, suddenly lost in his thoughts. Then he nodded and said, "It was white when I was a kid. Mom told me if the army ever tried to send me to a war, she would move us to Canada. To a farm in Alberta."

He smiled when he recalled this. She touched his face and told him they had to go. "Or I'll miss my train and you'll have to marry me instead of Paul."

ooooo

At the gate, Charlie put out his hand for her to shake. Instead she took him into her arms. People walking past them could easily have seen what neither of them saw: In her pale green eyes as she looked past him, and in his blue eyes as he looked past her, there was the same mix of desire and apprehension. Neither of them wanted to let go.

"Well," he finally said when he stepped away from her, "your flower girl is certainly going to look beautiful."

"Yes," she said. "Thank you."

"Maybe I—" he said, then stopped abruptly.

"What?" she asked him.

He looked down the tracks into the darkness. "Oh, I don't know, Sally."

She took his hand and told him that she didn't want to leave him. "I don't like the idea at all. And you have to tell me that you're not going to do anything silly again."

Now it was even more difficult for Charlie to look at her.

"I don't have any answers, Sally," he said.

She smiled at this. "The answers don't matter, Charlie," she told him. "There's so much that we can't know. We can't even look up at the sky and say how far it goes."

He smiled back at her. "True," he said.

"I'm going to try to earn this chance that you gave me," she told him.

He was dumbfounded. After all, she had saved his life. He watched her board the train. He wanted to tell her something, maybe just to thank her properly.

The train began to move with a sudden lurch. "Call your father," Sally said to him once more, and then he watched her disappear with a wave behind the sliding door.

EIGHT

*W*e tell ourselves that life is short, but actually, our lives take a long time to run out. We go on across many years, and there are some seasons that seem to last forever, nights that won't end, hours that we can barely endure. But at the end of our lives, when we look back, I wonder if most of it is just a blur. Except for those moments that gather intensity and clarity over the passage of time. Those few moments that seem to define our lives. I think those are the moments when we changed. Of course we couldn't feel that we were changing, but we were. We were leaving behind the person we had been and becoming someone new.

Charlie was changing that night as he walked out of Penn Station. On the sidewalk, the cold air shocked him. At a newsstand where he read the grim headlines of mortgage foreclosures and job layoffs, he pulled up the collar of his coat, then stuffed his hands into his pockets. He couldn't remember ever being colder in his life. He looked up at the cobalt sky, and where he had counted just seven stars before from the window ledge of the Waldorf, there were now millions. He turned until he found the North

Star. For years his father had told him a story about a night in Charlie's childhood when the two of them were out walking under the North Star. Charlie had pointed to it and said, "Daddy, you're older than me, so you're going to die first. But when you die, wait for me on that star so I can find you." Charlie remembered how his father's eyes always filled with tears whenever he told the story.

Tonight a halo encircled the star so that its light was faded, as if it were burning out. He kept his eyes on it, his head turned, as he walked along the sidewalk.

He came upon a Salvation Army stand where a woman smiled at him as she shook her silver bell. He passed her, then stopped and turned back. And when he had emptied his pockets and given her the last of his money, he took out his phone again and without thinking or making a decision, punched in his father's number. He was looking up at the star when the phone stopped ringing. "Pop?" he said. Then he heard Sally's voice, and he remembered.

"Charlie? Thank God you called. I forgot to give you back your father's phone. "

We can say, then, that this was the reason he ran to the curb and stopped the first taxi he saw. What he did next was beyond reason, really, and in order to understand it, we need to leave New York City just as the train was sailing across the moonlit countryside of New Jersey, where the whole world seemed to be sleeping as the snow began to fall again, this time on a strong wind that blew in off the Long Island Sound. If we are up high enough, just above the telephone poles and the church steeples, we can see the lighted bridges and the Manhattan skyline disappearing in the distance, and the bright light of the train's locomotive burrowing through the blowing snow, and the rectanglular windows of the train lit up like TV screens. And finally we can see a car's headlights moving very fast up the highway that runs parallel with the train tracks. And one more light on the roof of the car illuminating the word TAXI. And as the car draws even with the train, another light goes on, the interior light that illuminates Charlie's face in the back seat.

The taxi followed the train until it came to a stop at the little clapboard station in Princeton. Because there were no passengers waiting to board, only one conductor stepped out into the storm, and he quickly waved a flashlight signaling the engineer to pull away. He never saw Charlie running toward him through the blowing snow, but from her window, Sally saw him. She rushed to the open vestibule between the sleeper cars, and as he caught up with the train, she held his father's phone out for him. "I'm sorry, Charlie," she said. "How absentminded of me."

He didn't take the phone. By now the train was rolling

along slowly and he was jogging to keep up. "Here, Charlie," she said again as she reached towards him.

"I'm going with you to Chicago," he said. There wasn't time for her to say anything before he grabbed the railing and hauled himself in.

"Is it okay?" he asked when he was standing beside her.

There was a look of such confusion in his eyes that Sally took his hand to calm him. "Of course it's okay," she told him.

She showed him into the little room. The tiny sink and toilet, a chair at the window, the two small bunk beds that unfolded from the wall. "It's like a doll house," she said, as she took his coat and draped it over the chair. Then the train began to pick up speed. She watched Charlie steady himself with his hand on the window. When they rolled slowly past the station, they saw there was a lighted Christmas tree beside the tracks, a perfectly shaped tree with a gold star lit up on top. "I didn't see the tree there before," Charlie said.

"You were in a hurry," she said.

This explanation didn't seem to satisfy him. "No, I must have run right past it. It's strange," he said to himself as the train began to pick up speed. "I don't understand."

She climbed into the upper bunk and then called down to him. "How old are you, Charlie?

He looked up at her. "Thirty-one, next month," he said. "Remember, I told you?"

"Oh, I'm sorry," she said. "Of course. I just turned thirty," she told him. "I would have been married for three years by now if it hadn't been for this war. An old married lady, Charlie."

She leaned down from the top bunk and asked him if he was tired.

"Come to think of it," he said, "I guess I've never been this tired in my life."

"Let's sleep," she said.

He stretched out on the bunk below her. After a brief silence he said, "You haven't told me why you left California."

"It was Walt Whitman who brought us to New York," she said.

"Walt Whitman?"

"Paul's favorite poet. He wanted to write his poems where Whitman wrote. Then the war came."

She yawned deeply, then sang one line of a song, which was her ritual before falling asleep.

"Oh dear, bread and beer, if I were married, I wouldn't be here."

They didn't say another word. They lay with their heads on the tiny pillows, watching the snow blow past their window while their breathing filled the little room. Soon they were fast asleep, Charlie with the St. Christopher medallion in one closed fist, Sally with her hair sweeping across her cheek. They slept like children, dreaming the sweet dreams of the innocent while the train sailed across wide open land, not a building or road or tree in sight, beyond all the reference points that could lead them back to where their journey had begun.

Within an hour the train was flying through a blizzard blown in from the Northern Atlantic. Inside the locomotive, the chief engineer and his assistant were drinking hot chocolate from the dining car, when the phone rang with word that a freight train had jumped the tracks west of Albany. "After our stop in Stockbridge, they want us to head up into Canada and proceed to the west coast on the CP line," the engineer said.

"Been there. Done that," said the other man.

"Yep. It never goes over well with passengers who thought they were going to wake up in Chicago. Last time it happened, I had a fellow try to jump off the train."

The assistant shook his head and said he would notify the conductors. As he reached for the intercom, he peered out the window at the blowing snow. "Quite a damned storm," he said.

High winds had shaken the power lines to the ground in Stockbridge, and the station lights were out when the train pulled in just after midnight. They took on food and water, the yardmen working blind in the drifting snow and freezing cold. From the warmth of the locomotive, the engineer and his assistant watched them moving about like ghosts in the storm, both men grateful they were inside. Twenty minutes passed, and some brave soul intent upon doing his job ventured out from the station and passed a small canvas bag of mail on the end of a long pole up to the high window of the locomotive. The assistant opened it in the pale light and stared down at a Western Union telegram, trying to read the name in the little wax-paper window as they began moving slowly forward again, straining to pick up speed against the gale force wind.

"My God," he heard the engineer exclaim. He looked up and then out ahead where, through the blowing snow, he saw a figure huddled beside the tracks. "What do you make of that?" he said.

"A lost soul, I'd say, wouldn't you?" the engineer replied. They both watched until the figure disappeared in the storm.

A moment later, just as the caboose cleared the platform, the sky convulsed with a violent burst of lightning like a flair igniting. Sparks hissed from the electrical outlets in every car. Each window flashed brightly for two seconds. Resting on top of Charlie's folded overcoat on the upholstered chair by the window, his iPhone blinked its pulsing red light one last time, like a beating heart, then shut off.

BOOK II

*I*t was one of those nights that lasted forever, or only for a few moments. When Charlie opened his eyes, he couldn't tell how long he'd been sleeping, or if he'd fallen asleep at all. He awoke suddenly, jack-knifing up in his berth with the sense that someone was calling to him. The first thing he did was reach for his iPhone, and discovered that it was dead. He looked around the room and saw at once that something was wrong. Sally's eight-sided box from the bridal shop was no longer on the chair by the window. He jumped to his feet, slamming his head on the bunk above him, which was now empty and neatly made. He ran his hand over the pillow. He breathed on the window, cleared a small opening in the frost with the flat of his hand, and peered out into the night. All that was visible was a white world reaching far into the distance. He pushed the power button on his phone again and nothing happened. He shook the phone. Still nothing. He seemed mildly confused, and as he slid it into his pocket, he glanced down at the floor and saw a Western Union envelope lying there. He picked it up hesitantly and read Sally's name. For a moment he thought of opening the telegram and reading it, but then he slipped it into his shirt pocket and went out of the room to look for her.

He unlatched the metal door and pushed it open to a dimly lit corridor. He looked in both directions and saw no one. He began walking slowly to a lighted door that led into another car. He felt the rocking motion of the train through the soles of his feet. When he pushed open the door and stepped into the next car, he saw that every seat was taken by a sleeping passenger, many of them snoring. He made his way slowly up the aisle, looking from side to side at these people, whom he imagined were heading home for the holidays. It took a few moments before he realized they were all soldiers in uniform. Some had a small American flag sewn over their hearts, others a Canadian flag. Above each man in the overhead rack was a dark green duffle bag. He remembered how tired he had felt a few hours before, though he couldn't say how many hours he had slept, but these soldiers looked truly exhausted. They seemed to have exceeded any definition of weariness. They slept like old men, but when Charlie studied their faces he saw they were very young, all of them soldiers in uniforms of World War II. On one man's lap was a newspaper lying open. The *New York Tribune*, dated December 19, 1945. In another soldier's folded hands was a photograph of a pregnant young woman standing on the front lawn of a little house, smiling at the camera. Another soldier had fallen asleep holding a Hallmark Christmas card and a pen he was using to write inside the card. Charlie had almost made his way to the door of the next car when he turned and looked back. He retraced his steps to the soldier with the newspaper and as he stood looking down at the date-line, he felt a strange sensation below his feet. More than the movement of the train, he seemed to feel the velocity falling out of his life. Very carefully, he placed his hand on the newspaper, as if making sure it was real. And then he found himself almost running up the aisle, with the curiosity of a child, to the door of the next car.

The instant he pushed open the door, he heard the sounds of laughter and loud voices, and a radio playing one of those old Swing numbers that his father and mother had danced the jitterbug to in the kitchen when he was a small boy.

Soldiers were drinking and talking at a bar. They barely seemed to notice him when he walked past them. Above the bar was a poster of President Franklin D. Roosevelt under the words BUY WAR BONDS. As he stared at the poster, Charlie began to feel cold, as if the winter storm raging outside the train had entered him. He looked back up at the poster to the face of FDR. He remembered his history well enough to recall how this man had spent seven years learning to stand up in iron leg braces to give the appearance of walking after polio paralyzed him, because he wanted to become president of the United States and knew he wouldn't be elected if he was in a wheelchair. Charlie was about to order a drink from the bartender when he heard someone call to him. "Charlie, Hurry up, son."

He turned and saw a poker game in progress at a table by the window. There were four soldiers in the game, and one old fellow with a wrinkled face and a jaunty hat that had a PRESS I.D. pinned to it. The old fellow looked up and gestured to the empty chair beside him. "Come on, Charlie. Time is money."

Charlie wasn't processing any of this very quickly; his brain was lagging behind the events. But the empty seat at the table was obviously his. And there was a huge pile of money in front of the empty seat. It was obviously his as well. Charlie walked to the table and sat down.

"You don't look so good, Charlie," the old timer said. "Where did you go?"

Before he could answer, another soldier said, "You were about to tell us how you managed to stay out of the damned war."

There was a silence, and then all the soldiers turned and looked at Charlie. He felt his throat go dry, and the top of his head burned as if someone had set fire to his hair. And then the perfect lie came to him.

"I have a farm in Alberta, Canada," he improvised with absolute conviction.

One of the soldiers added, "For a farmer from Alberta you're one hell of a poker player."

Charlie just nodded. Another soldier spoke. "I know a farmer from home. He didn't have to go fight either. Somebody has to stay home and grow the food. Fair enough."

"I had you pegged for a farmer," the man in the absurd PRESS hat said.

"And who are you?" Charlie asked.

"Who am I? Very funny, Charlie. How could you forget my name, after all the money you've taken from me. Johnny. Remember?"

One soldier raised a bottle of beer in a drunken toast. "Here's to Mary who lives on the hill, what she won't do, her sister will. Here's to her sister!"

As soon as he finished, he fell from his seat and passed out on the floor.

Charlie got to his feet, preparing to leave.

"Sit, Charlie," Johnny said to him. "You've won most of our money. The least you can do is give us a chance to win some of it back."

It was a big pile of money, and for a moment Charlie was transfixed by it. He took his seat in front of it, like a man cast suddenly in a spell, and despite himself, began counting it. Johnny lit a cigar and then handed one to Charlie, as he started to deal the next hand. "Straight five-card stud. Read 'em and weep, soldiers."

Then Charlie remembered Sally's empty bunk and the feeling he'd had a few moments before, the feeling that he might never see her again. "I'm looking for someone," he said.

"Is her name Betty?" a soldier asked him.

"Betty? No," he said with surprise.

"I'm looking for Betty," the soldier said. "Betty Grable."

Everyone at the table laughed.

Charlie turned to Johnny again. "What newspaper did you say you write for?" he questioned him.

Johnny didn't miss a beat. He continued dealing as he replied. "*Boston Herald*. Just got back from Manheim, Germany. Covering the death of poor old General George Patton. 'Old Blood and Guts.' Tuesday I was in the nation's capital when Congress voted to join the United Nations. Last Monday, I was following a lead about the eight Navy airmen who disappeared in the Bermuda Triangle."

"You get around," Charlie said, picking up his cards. Then he whispered to Johnny, "so, is this some movie you're making here? You're just waiting for the cameras?"

"Yes, I do get around, son," Johnny replied. "I'm an old bloodhound, always looking for a good story."

Charlie warily eyed his cards. When he got to the last one, he discovered that a sixth card was stuck behind it. An ace. Just what he needed to complete a full house, if he was willing to cheat and not give back the extra card. He looked around the table, considering what he would do. And then he thought, Why look a gift horse in the mouth? He hid the card he had substituted for the ace, a six of clubs, and won the hand with his full house.

"A full house with five cards," one soldier remarked. "You don't see that every day."

"You certainly don't," Johnny quipped.

Charlie nodded and smiled.

That was just the beginning. Soon he was hitting his stride, winning hand after hand. He felt his luck changing with each pot he won; it felt like the easiest money he'd ever made, or stolen, in his life. He chomped down on his cigar and his eyes lit up as he began to enjoy himself for the first time in months.

"You've got all the luck, farmer," Johnny told him. "So what do you grow on that farm of yours in Alberta?"

Charlie gave him a long look as the answer came to him from another century. "I grow corn," he said. "Lots of corn."

Johnny called to the bartender for another bottle. Then he leaned close to Charlie and whispered in his ear. "I thought for sure you were going to ask me the question, son."

Charlie wasn't paying attention. Instead he was watching the cards being dealt for the next hand.

"What question?" he asked distractedly.

"Most people ask me the same question," Johnny went on. "They want to know why he made a dog's life so short."

None of the other soldiers at the poker table were paying attention to Johnny, but by now Charlie was. He regarded him with mounting suspicion. "No kidding?" he said.

"I kid you not, Charlie. That's what most people want to know. Because it's so sad, I guess, the way dogs grow old so much faster than people do. I'll give you my stock answer: It's not fair. Life isn't fair, right?"

"You can say that again."

"Yeah, you're right. And we should be grateful that it isn't fair, or you and I would be six feet under ground right now with all the poor souls who fought and died in this bloody war, instead of riding the rails on such a heavenly night as this. Right? Am I right?"

That got Charlie's attention, but only momentarily, before he turned back to the card game. One of the soldiers said to him, "So, you didn't have to serve in the Canadian army because you had to run the family farm. What's that work like?"

Charlie's lie had worked like a charm, and this gave him confidence to keep on lying. If there was one thing he had learned as a Wall Street broker it was to sling the bull, and he had the feeling that if he played along it might work to his advantage. "What's it like? Well, it's no picnic getting up at four every morning."

Now, with a certain measure of satisfaction, Johnny watched Charlie weave his web. First, he had cheated at cards, and now he was proving himself to be an exemplary liar.

"What the hell is there to do at four in the morning?" one soldier asked as he looked over his cards.

Charlie said the first thing that came into his head. "Shovel manure, I guess."

The soldier laughed. "What do you mean, you guess?"

"Sounds like a great way to start the day," a third soldier put in.

"Like latrine duty," said another.

"What kind of manure, Charlie?" Johnny asked.

One of the soldiers said, "One kind is just as bad as the other, if you ask me."

"Actually," Charlie joined in, " all manure is not created equal. I specialize in pig manure. There's a certain sweetness to it." All the soldiers at the table laughed, and Johnny listened and smiled to himself with satisfaction. They were all having a fine time, and it pleased Charlie to look around and see that he had won over this crowd so easily. It made him feel that maybe he still had a certain power, that same power that had served him so well as he worked his way up at the brokerage firm. He picked up his cards from the table. Another great hand. "Who's betting first, boys?" he said jauntily.

ooooo

It went on that way, happily, for several hours as the train bore through the dark, snowy night and all the money placed on the table somehow ended up in front of Charlie, and he forgot where he was and didn't care about anything but the pile of cash in front of him. It was the easiest money he had ever made, and the fact that he was winning again at something had an intoxicating effect, so that the hours at the poker table seemed to pass in minutes.

Eventually it came to an end when he had won all the money the others had. "You cleaned us out, Charlie," Johnny said, still smiling that enthusiastic little grin.

"I'm tapped out," one of the soldiers said.

"You're one hell of a lucky farmer," another told him. "If I was you, I'd get out of farming completely and play poker for a living. Stop shoveling manure and just shovel in the dough instead."

Charlie acknowledged all of this with a shrug and a little self-deprecating wave of his hand as he began counting his winnings once more.

He was almost finished, when he exclaimed with his cigar clamped between his teeth, "After I get some sleep maybe we'll play again." He looked up then and saw that he was alone. All the soldiers were gone. The light over the bar had been turned off, and the bartender himself was nowhere to be seen. He had been so enthralled by his winnings that he hadn't said goodnight to anyone.

Suddenly Charlie was seized by a deep and terrible loneliness. It was as if all the windows on the train had broken and the bitter cold storm raging outside was now within. He felt ice on his spine and a dull ache in his chest. And when he turned slightly, he caught an unexpected glimpse of his reflection in the glass sitting in front of his pile of money. All his adult life he had never been able to look at himself in the mirror without fussing a little with his hair, worrying that he might be losing it, but now as he leaned close to the glass and raised his hand reflexively, he stopped short when the face staring back at him looked so old and tired that he could see his father in the shadows around his eyes, and the furrows across his forehead. It was as if his old man were outside the window looking in at him. "What the hell ever happened to you?" Charlie said bitterly. Then he turned away and tried to figure out how to carry all his money.

TEN

*H*e made a sack from the white linen tablecloth, and it was slung over his shoulder when he kicked open the door to the vestibule between two cars and almost walked into a soldier standing there, alone, smoking and looking off into the distance. He had an angry look in his eyes that matched the bitterness Charlie felt. "Watch where you're going, Santa Claus," he said, glaring at Charlie, then turning away to resume his solitary vigil.

Charlie apologized, but the soldier didn't acknowledge this. He had returned to his own thoughts and as he gazed into the darkness and the blowing snow, he began drumming his hand against his leg, as if he was keeping time to some beat in his head. When he took a pint bottle from his coat pocket and gulped its contents like he was dying of thirst, it gave Charlie the chills, unnerving him so that he apologized a second time. The soldier turned and faced him and said, "What's a guy got to do to get some privacy around here?"

Charlie heard himself speaking anxiously. "My old man was in the war," he said. "I don't know where he fought, or anything. He never talked about it."

The man gave Charlie a baleful expression. "So what?" he said. Then he threw his cigarette out into the darkness, turned his back to Charlie, pushed open the door to the next car, and walked away.

"Good riddance," Charlie said under his breath when the door had swung shut. Before he could take his next step, the door swung back open and the soldier was standing in front of him again, jaw to jaw. "What did you just say to me?" He sneered.

This is all just a bad dream, Charlie thought. None of this is really happening. "Nothing," he replied. "I was talking to myself."

The soldier's eyes narrowed. "You bore me," he said as he stomped off.

From there, Charlie walked quickly through three more cars until he found the door to his room. The encounter with the soldier had shaken him so that he could no longer remember the final tally of the money he'd won. And so he dropped to his knees, opened the sack, and started counting again. He didn't hear Johnny come up behind him.

"I already added it up, kid," he said.

Charlie was so startled that his cigar tumbled towards the floor. Johnny caught it in mid-air across his shoe. "Take a guess how much it will be worth sixty-four years from now," he said sternly.

Charlie looked up like an elementary school student being scolded by his teacher. As sure as he had been that no one had seen him cheating in the poker game, he was now just as sure that Johnny had him nailed.

"Adjusted for inflation, four hundred seventy-seven thousand, five hundred and fourteen dollars," Johnny said. "Does that figure ring a bell, kid?" He stared hard at Charlie. "Come on kid," he egged him on, "you're supposed to be good with numbers."

Finally Charlie spoke, but he was too defeated to raise his voice above a whisper. "That was the amount of my dad's pension."

"Which you lost," Johnny said.

Charlie could only nod his head in shame.

"So, let me get this straight now, kid," Johnny went on. "You're standing here outside the door and you've got a choice—you can open it and see if your girl has returned, or you can count your money." For emphasis, he reached down into Charlie's sack and grabbed a fistful of bills. "That's your choice, Charlie. The girl with real blood running through her, or paper." He leaned closer to Charlie. "You chose paper," he said solemnly. "Some men step outside at night before they go to sleep and look up at the stars. Others count their money. I've always thought that women fall in love with the first kind, marry the second kind, and spend the rest of their lives dreaming about the first kind. You've got the look on your face of a man who's wondering whether or not the Tokyo Exchange is going to open strong."

"Old habit," Charlie said glumly. And that was when what Johnny had said hit him. He felt his defiance returning. "That's very quaint, okay, about the guy looking up at the stars at night, very quaint indeed, but why don't you lay your cards on the table, mister, and tell me what kind of trick you're playing here?"

"I'm not sure I understand," Johnny said.

"What are you, some kind of hypnotist?" Charlie went on. "How would you know about the Tokyo Exchange?"

"Too bad you never owned a dog, Charlie. A dog could have taught you an awful lot about humility."

"I don't need any lessons in humility after the last six months. I don't know what world you come from, but let me tell you, the world I live in is falling to pieces."

"I understand," Johnny said.

"You understand? How could you understand?"

"I've been around, kid."

"Yeah, I guess you have. Real bloodhound for a good story and all that crap."

"Most people miss the real story."

Charlie wasn't listening. He was too busy composing in his head what he wanted to say next, too busy to recognize that this was precisely what Sally had told him at the Waldorf when he was standing in the open window. "You want to hear a story? I'll tell you a story. I played by the rules ever since I was a kid. Homework right after school. First in my class. And nothing came easily to me, okay? I grew up in a trailer park in Hoboken, New Jersey, with a father who drank like booze was going out of style. I worked my butt off to get into Princeton. And then Harvard. They don't just let you into those places because you're fun to play golf with. You have to earn your way, and I earned mine, believe me, I earned my way. I wore the right clothes and shook the right hands and signed on the dotted line. And then it was my turn. Do you hear me? It was my turn to really make . . . to make something of myself." He took a deep breath. "Instead, I woke up one morning and found that nothing was the way I always thought it was. I'd been tricked, you understand? So I don't need any more tricks from you."

He had gotten a lot off his chest and was suddenly exhausted. He felt like he was running out of steam. And so was the train. It began to slow, and both men turned and saw a small station coming into view through the blowing snow.

"Thanks for telling me your story, kid," Johnny said. "Maybe someday if we meet again, I'll tell you an even better one about a guy who got everything he wanted, and then learned the meaning of life when he let go of the thing he wanted most."

With that he tipped his silly hat, stepped across the corridor, and threw open the door.

"Wait," Charlie said.

"Make sure you deliver the telegram," Johnny said, pointing to Charlie's shirt pocket as he prepared to jump from the train.

Charlie took it from his pocket and threw it on the floor. "I'm getting off with you," he said. "I have to get back to New York."

"What about your girl?" Johnny asked.

"I already told you, she's not my girl. She's engaged to a soldier. And she's not on this train anyway. This isn't real. None of this is real."

"Well, look at the telegram. That's real, isn't it?"

Suddenly Charlie didn't know what to say. He felt like a little boy again and Johnny seemed to feel sorry for him. "Maybe you'll get lucky, kid," he said. "Maybe her soldier isn't coming home from the war. You'll get the girl and the money. How would you like that?"

Charlie answered slowly, his defiance now replaced by utter exhaustion. "I think I want to disappear," he said, as he picked up the telegram and slid it back into his pocket.

"Check out, you mean?"

"Yeah, I think so," he answered.

This made Johnny impatient. "These people who disappear because they can't take it anymore, do you know what happens to them, kid? They don't stick around long enough to find out why they were here. I don't have much sympathy for them, to tell you the truth. Not when you consider what some parents have to go through with sick children." He kicked the door shut and began running toward the station.

"Hey!" Charlie yelled. "You haven't told me what's going on here!" He tried to turn the handle to open the door, but it was stuck. Even when he kicked the handle with his foot, it wouldn't turn. Finally he kicked it so hard that it broke off and fell to the floor. By then the train was picking up speed, and all Charlie could do was look out the window and see Johnny receding down the tracks. His last glimpse of him was standing on the snow-covered platform beside a beautiful lighted Christmas tree with a perfect gold star at its peak, an exact duplicate of the tree he had seen at the station in Princeton. And Johnny was waving back at Charlie, who was growing more frustrated by the second. It was freezing cold with his head out the window, but when he tried to turn back inside, he discovered that he was hooked on something and couldn't get his head in. He began talking to himself in a kind of desperate soliloquy. "Oh, that's great. Just great, you loser. What kind of idiot gets his head stuck out the window of a moving train?" He was trying as hard as he could to extricate himself, growing more and more frustrated and confused. And then things got worse. Much worse. Up ahead was a freight train hurrying towards him on the adjacent track. It was going to be close. He had maybe two minutes to get free. Okay, he said to himself. Okay, be calm.

He could turn his head just far enough to look back and see the lighted Christmas tree, way off in the distance now. He closed his eyes and tried to remember what it was to pray. "Okay," he said to himself. "I give up. I surrender." Saying this, he was overcome by a sudden calm that ran through him. It didn't matter very much that he was going to be beheaded. Nothing mattered, as all the frustration and despair of the past year drained out of him. And when he opened his eyes, he saw that he was hooked to the window latch by the St. Christopher medallion that Sally had given him in the Waldorf, in what seemed like another life. He looked once more at the oncoming train, and then back at the necklace, working at it calmly until, at last, he was free and safely back inside the window just before the freight train thundered past.

s Charlie turned to his door, he saw Sally coming toward him, strikingly dressed in a long, pale blue cashmere topcoat with a matching beret, an elegant black scarf, and high heels. She looked like an international diplomat en route to an assignment in Paris. She carried a leather suitcase in one hand and in the other, the lovely eight-sided box from the bridal shop. Beside her on crutches, and also dressed beautifully in a dark green cloth coat, was a little girl, five or six years old.

They stopped short when they saw Charlie. His face and hair were caked with ice and snow. And he stared at them with wide eyes as if he were beholding an apparition. He could tell by Sally's expression that she had no idea who he was.

"Can we help you?" she asked him sweetly.

He recognized her voice, and the calm surrender of the confession that had followed his brush with death was replaced by his old defiance. "Can you help me? I was almost decapitated three minutes ago. And what about you? Where in God's name did you go, and who's she?"

Sally took a half step away, that showed him he had frightened her. "I'm sorry," she said softly. "Scarlet and I just got on the train. The conductor told us that the only empty bed is in your room." She gestured to his door.

The child stepped towards him on her crutches and held out her hand for him to shake, which he ignored.

He shook the snow from his head and exclaimed, "We have to get off this train and get back to New York. We can get married there."

The child tilted her head to one side. "Sally's already getting married," she said. "And you look like Santa Claus."

Charlie looked at Sally. When he saw no recognition in her eyes, he slumped to the floor, defeated again.

Sally spoke next. "You're riding as far as Alberta?"

He looked up at her. "Where did you go?" he asked her.

She shook her head. "I don't understand," she said. "Maurice told us that you were returning to your farm in Canada."

Charlie looked deeply into her eyes. "I don't think this train goes anywhere near Canada," he said. "And who the heck is Maurice?"

"We're in Canada already, sir," the child said.

Charlie looked numbly out the dark window, as if he might see something through the blowing snow to confirm or deny this.

"What do you grow on your farm?" the little girl asked him.

Before Charlie answered, he looked at Sally's face again for some explanation, but seeing only her confusion, he knew they would believe whatever he told them. "Corn," he said dejectedly. "Mostly corn."

"I like corn," the child announced brightly.

"I hate it," Charlie said.

The child stepped close to him. "A lot of people who came to the orphanage wanted to adopt me," she told him. "They wanted a little girl with polio. But Sally wanted me the most."

Sally was looking at him and waiting for what he would say. He just nodded his head and kept silent.

"I'm sleepy," the child told him.

He knelt down and she laid her head on his shoulder. He had never been this close to a child before, and he felt most awkward. Then she whispered. "Do you know what happens when we die?"

He was astonished and it took a moment for him to reply. "No," he said, "I'm sorry, I don't."

"Me neither," she said. "I wonder if anybody does."

Charlie reached up and pushed open the door to his room.

"It's all yours," he said, gesturing for them to enter. He followed behind, then closed the door and slumped miserably to the floor, wedged between the window and the upholstered chair. He turned away from them and made a pillow for his head from his sack of money.

TWELVE

*F*or a long time, Charlie lay on the floor listening to them breathe. At first he could distinguish one from the other as the child took shorter breaths, nearly two of hers for each one of Sally's, but sometime before he closed his eyes, their breathing merged into a single rhythmic pattern that somehow matched the evenly spaced clacking of the train's iron wheels as it rattled along the rails. The last thought Charlie had when he closed his eyes was that Sally and the child would be gone by morning and that he would be alone again, a prisoner in this cramped room with its ice-covered window, with no memory of ever stepping onto the train, but condemned to ride it forever through an unrelenting snowstorm.

He awoke to the first light of morning, a pale gray haze that lay muted against the window. He was freezing. His joints were so cold that when he raised his arms and then rose to his feet, he felt afflicted with arthritis. Sally and the child had shared the upper bunk and he saw their breath turning to white frost in the icy air. Their faces were colorless in the cold, as if they were no longer alive, and he quickly pulled his blankets and sheets from the lower berth and covered them. Then he spread their coats over the blankets before he left the room.

He made his way through one car of sleeping soldiers, swaying and lurching as he walked. In the open vestibule between cars he stepped through a snowdrift up to his waist. "What we need is a little more snow!" he complained, his voice interrupting the silence of the next car, where many wounded soldiers lay on gurneys that had replaced all the seats. A Red Cross nurse attending to one patient whose head was wrapped in white bandages looked up at him with accusing eyes. By now Charlie felt like an intruder and he could barely get out his question: "Which way is the bar?"

The nurse looked for a moment like she was going to oblige him by pointing the direction, but then returned to the wounded soldier without answering. Charlie turned slightly and saw that another soldier was staring at him. "Have a drink for me," the fellow said. It wasn't until Charlie had waved to him amicably that he noticed both of the man's sleeves were empty and laying flatly at his sides. "Make it a scotch and soda," the soldier called before he closed his eyes. Charlie felt himself struggling to move forward. The next thing his eyes focused on was a short length of red rubber hose disappearing into another man's stomach. This took Charlie's breath away, making him feel like he was back on the window ledge of the Waldorf, gasping for air in the swirling wind. It was almost too much for him to bear. He longed to be at the poker table with Johnny and the others. Instead he felt surrounded by ghosts who seemed reluctant to release him. It was only after a great effort that he felt the door at the far end of the car opening beneath the flat of his hand.

Immediately he heard the clinking of china. Out ahead, an elderly man with a dyed-red moustache, matching sideburns, and a red bow tie danced his way from table to table, laying down the place settings. "*Bon matin, monsieur,*" he called to Charlie without missing a beat. "You must be the farmer from Alberta. I am Maurice."

Charlie stepped towards him, asking, "Why do you say that?"

Maurice stopped his work long enough to explain. "Because, monsieur, you and I are the only two men on this train who are not in uniform. I was too old to fight in the war, and you were excused to run your family's farm, I have heard."

"Who told you that?" Charlie asked stiffly.

Maurice gave him a long look. "It was Johnny."

"Johnny got off the train."

"*Mais, oui,* you are right, but we spoke before he got off. As a matter of fact, he told me to tell you the reason the dear Lord made a dog's life so much shorter than a man's is so that the dog can show us what it will be like for us when we grow old."

He cocked his head and walked away the length of the car, through a door at the far end with an oval glass window. After a moment's hesitation, Charlie followed him, his anger mounting again with each step. Finally he burst through the door and charged into a kitchen that consisted of two black wood-fired cookstoves that faced each other across a narrow aisle, steel sinks, and racks of pots and pans. "Look, mister," Charlie began, his voice entering the room just ahead of him. "I don't know who you are, but I'm not a farmer from Alberta. I need to get to New York. When does this train stop so I can get off?"

Maurice had his head inside an oven. "Parry Sound, Ontario, in eighteen hours," he called back to Charlie.

"Eighteen hours," Charlie said bitterly. "Well, can you give me something to eat, I'm starving."

Maurice removed himself from the oven and pointed at Charlie's shirt pocket.

"What?" Charlie snarled.

"You haven't given the mademoiselle her telegram, I see."

Charlie took it from his pocket. "Where did this come from, anyway?" He shook the envelope in the old man's face. "Were you behind this? Yeah, I'll bet you and Johnny are behind this whole charade."

"Charade, monsieur?"

"That's what I said. A ruse. A trick. Someone is playing a trick on me."

"A folly?" Maurice said. "Do you know what is man's great folly?"

"Do I know man's great folly? What kind of absurd question is that?" Charlie barked back at him.

Maurice only smiled with satisfaction. "It is only my opinion, monsieur. You may take it or leave it, as you please. Every man with half a brain knows the folly: When he reaches the end of his life, a man will wish that every hour he spent tending his lawn he had spent making love to his wonderful wife. And yet when he opens his eyes on a Saturday morning and his beautiful wife is asleep beside him, all he can think about is his lawn mower waiting for him in the garage."

"Very funny," Charlie said. "For your information, I don't have a wife or a damned lawn."

"But someday, monsieur, you will have both."

"How do you know?"

Maurice didn't answer. Instead he said, "Perhaps you should open the telegram."

"It's not for me, so why would I do that?" Charlie said.

"Because it is for the young woman who means something to you. And I can tell you from experience that, since this war began, these telegrams always carry bad news."

Charlie looked down at the telegram and slowly withdrew it from his pocket.

"You see, *mon ami*, if this is terrible news for your friend, it would be much better if you are the one to tell her."

Charlie thought about this, both surprised and disappointed in himself that he was even considering opening Sally's telegram. But what the old man was saying made some sense.

"Perhaps we should execute a test," Maurice said with a look of resignation.

"What do you mean?" Charlie asked.

"Surely you've tested God before, monsieur."

"I don't know what you're talking about."

"Any kind of test, sir. If the telephone rings in the next ten minutes, then I am meant to do this or that. If I see a shooting star in the sky tonight, then this means that God wants me to return home. You see?"

Charlie shook his head and began to walk away.

"Monsieur, I think you should consider what I am saying, even if you believe that I am a lunatic."

Charlie turned around and faced him. Maurice's hands were open at his sides. "We don't have to call it God if this offends you, we can call it Fate. You believe in Fate don't you?"

"It depends," Charlie said. "What's the test?"

"It could be anything, monsieur. What if I put my hands behind my back and you try to guess what number I am making. Two fingers. Five fingers, whatever."

"Go ahead," Charlie said.

The man put his hands behind his back. "I am ready," he said.

"Four," Charlie said.

Maurice smiled and withdrew his hands, showing two fingers opened on each hand. "Well, well, well," he said slowly.

"Well, well, well," Charlie mocked him. "You cheated."

Maurice straightened his shoulders and announced theatrically, "I cheat neither man nor God."

"Okay," Charlie said, "let's do it this way. You turn around, and I'll turn around, and on the count of three we'll face each other and we'll both throw out our hands."

Maurice nodded his approval and said, "That will work."

The first time they did it they both chose six. Then nine. Then three. Then seven. They were both out of breath when they finished, their faces just inches apart.

At last when Charlie seemed satisfied, Maurice said, "I believe God wants you to open the telegram now, monsieur."

Charlie just nodded his head. He didn't have any

resistance left in him. He held the telegram in his hands and looked down at Sally's name. Then he hesitated. "She's going to be somebody else's wife," he said. "What am I to her? She doesn't even know who I am."

Maurice gave him an understanding look. "You could be her friend, monsieur. In this world, you can always find another husband, or lover. But I have discovered that a friend is something much harder to find."

Charlie ran his fingers through his hair and looked at Maurice, who was doing the same thing, as if the way they had matched numbers in the game now placed them somehow on the same plane of existence. When Maurice realized this, he dropped his hand to his side and looked slightly embarrassed. "Well, monsieur," he said, "at least now we know."

"Know what?" Charlie said, his words seeming to startle him.

"What God wants you to do," he said. "Or what Fate has brought you here to do."

Charlie grimaced. I'm a fool, he thought. "Do you know where I was before I got on this train?"

"No, monsieur."

Charlie spoke in precise and measured syllables. "I was standing on the window ledge of the twenty-second floor of the Waldorf Astoria Hotel in New York City. I was going to end my life."

Before the old man could say anything, Charlie turned and began to walk away.

"But you didn't," Maurice called after him. "And that is why you are here."

THIRTEEN

*A*s Charlie passed through the vestibule outside the dining car, he saw the drumming soldier there alone again, smoking and staring into the early dawn at the blowing snow while he tapped his right hand against his thigh in a steady beat. Charlie didn't feel like talking and he walked right past him. But before he reached the next door, the soldier called to him. "So, what kind of father was he?"

"What did you say?" Charlie asked when he turned back.

"Your old man? What kind of father was he to you?"

"A drunk," Charlie said angrily. "Just what I deserved."

Before Charlie reached the door, the soldier called to him.

"My band was called The Renegades," he said.

This was enough to make Charlie walk back to him. "You were in a band?" he asked.

"Yep," the soldier said. He looked down at his right hand and said, "I was the drummer."

Charlie stood beside him now in the open vestibule, the snow blowing on both of them through the warming sunlight.

"I used to hear the music in my head," he continued. "My lead was Eddie Black. His mom was Puerto Rican. Eddie died in Anzio. Bobby Krum was our bass. He was a big clown. Six feet, six inches tall, two hundred and eighty pounds. You should have seen him hit a baseball. He got his head blown off on Omaha Beach. After our lead singer, Tom Lansdale, was killed in Belgium, I stopped hearing music. I don't hear our old songs anymore now."

He stopped and took a pint bottle from his coat pocket, drank from it, and offered it to Charlie.

"Too early for me," Charlie declined.

"I picked this up in Poland last week. It was good whiskey but I've just been refilling it with the cheap stuff from the bar. So, what do you want?"

"I don't know what you mean," Charlie answered.

"What is it you want from this lousy life?"

Charlie replied without hesitation. "I want to get back to New York, put some money in my bank that I won playing poker, for my dad."

The soldier gave Charlie a long, appraising look. "For your dad, huh?"

"Yeah."

"All I wanted was to get home in one piece or to be killed outright. Either one. I just didn't want to be wounded and come home a cripple. So here I am." He paused and took a long look at the whiskey bottle. "All the words are in Polish. I don't know what kind of whiskey it was, but it sure was good."

Charlie wasn't really listening to him. "I lost all my old man's money, and now I've got it back."

The soldier wasn't really listening to Charlie either. He was looking down the tracks. "It will be below zero tonight. I figure once I fall asleep in the snow I'll be dead in about an hour. The blood becomes too thick for the heart to pump. Simple."

Charlie watched the man shiver as a vacant cast fell over his eyes. "So you're planning to off yourself?"

The soldier took a cigarette from his pocket, lit it, and said, "I'm not going home."

Charlie thought about this for a moment. "Where are you from?" he asked the man.

"I don't talk about where I'm from. I don't even think about it anymore."

Charlie watched as the man took one last gulp of whiskey, draining the pint bottle, which he then slipped into his pocket as his eyes filled with sorrow. "I never had to fight a war," Charlie said. "But I always told myself that if I had to, I would climb a tree and hide there."

"No, you wouldn't," the soldier said. "You'd be afraid to hide. You'd be afraid of what people would say about you. Besides, there's no place to hide when the shells start exploding."

"You should go home," Charlie told him with a conviction that surprised both of them. He waited for the soldier to say something and when he didn't, he just kept talking to him. "Let me tell you something," he continued. "No matter what happened to you in the war, you're going home to a country that is grateful. All your life, no matter how bad things get for you, no matter what you lose, you'll be able to hold on to your self-respect and your dignity. No one will ever be able to take from you what you've accomplished."

"People will forget this war," the soldier said defiantly.

"Trust me," Charlie countered, "they aren't going to forget. And America is going to do things for you. You're going to get to go to college, and buy a house. And you're going to have kids, a whole army of kids. I'm telling you, it's a great time to be what you are—a soldier coming home from war. You did something really good in your life. A lot of people never get to say that."

As soon as Charlie finished speaking, the train ground to a slow stop like a great bull gored and brought to its knees in the ring.

"I wonder what's going on?" Charlie said.

They both looked down the tracks and saw a mountain of snow, twenty feet high, ahead across the rails. A moment later soldiers began jumping off the train with shovels.

"I doubt if there's a fitness room on this train," Charlie said. "I might as well get some exercise."

"You do that," the soldier said to him.

Before Charlie jumped down from the train, he shook the man's hand. "I'm sorry about the guys in your band," he said.

"They were my only friends," the man said.

FOURTEEN

*C*harlie had stripped off his coat and was soaked in sweat after an hour. For a long time he worked without talking to the others at all. He felt despair rising through him, as it had when he made the plan to end his life. In the dark months and weeks of the economic collapse he had run the gauntlet of emotions, first feeling that he was merely unlucky, then ultimately doomed by some nameless force. He felt that way again as he shoveled and beads of sweat ran down his face.

"Ah, trust me, fellows," he listened to one man saying. "There's a better world coming."

"I hope so," another soldier replied. "My mom died of something called cancer while I was gone."

Gradually Charlie lost himself in the physical work and the soldiers' chatter; then, one big-shouldered man the others called Chief climbed to the top of the mountain of snow and delivered a speech while they took a cigarette break. "Back in 1855, the chief of my people wrote a letter to President Franklin Pierce, after the president had asked to buy some of the tribe's land. The letter goes like this: 'The President in Washington sends word that he wishes to buy our land. But how can you buy or sell the sky? The idea is strange to us. If we do not own the freshness of the air and the sparkle of the water, how can you buy them. Every part of this earth is sacred to my people. Every shining pine needle, every sandy shore, every mist in the dark woods, every meadow, every humming insect. All are held in the memory and the experience of my people. We know the sap that courses through the trees as we know the blood that courses through our veins. If we sell you our land, remember that the air is precious to us, and that the air shares its spirit with all the life it supports. The wind that gave our grandfather his first breath also receives his last sigh. Each ghostly reflection in the clear waters of the lakes tells of events and memories in the life of my people. The water's murmur is the voice of my father's father.' "

To Charlie's surprise, he felt the man's words entering him. He felt like he was listening to words that had been whispered to him long ago by someone he trusted and loved. They were words that swept him away to a broad, open place that he could not identify, a place where he was small but not insignificant. He couldn't recall ever hearing anything more beautiful.

Just before the soldier climbed down, he said, "That was Chief Seattle. They named Seattle after him, but no

Indians were ever allowed into the city, and so he never saw the place that bore his name."

A few moments later they were all back at work again.

"Don't look now, Governor," one soldier called to Charlie, "but that beautiful girl of yours and her kid have been watching you."

Charlie turned slowly and regarded their faces at a window. "She's not my girl," he said. "She's going to California to marry a soldier just back from the war."

"She waited for him, then," the man said. "He's lucky. My girl gave up on me a year ago. I got a 'Dear John' letter when I was holed up on the side of a mountain in Italy. Was just about the worst night of my life, thinking about her with some other guy."

He stopped and looked at Charlie. "You look cold," he said.

"Yeah, it's cold," Charlie said, shivering again now that he had stopped shoveling.

"You think this is cold, you should have been at Bastogne. For the rest of my life, whenever it's cold I'm going to think of Bastogne."

"Her little girl must have polio," another soldier called to Charlie.

"I don't know, really," Charlie said.

"Well, she looks like a tough little kid," he remarked. "If there's one thing this war taught me, it's that we're all a hell of a lot tougher than we think we are. We whipped Hitler, Mussolini, and the Emperor of Japan in four years, and if my grandmother had been in uniform we'd have won the war in half the time. There's a woman, let me tell you. Raised seven kids, ran a potato farm, always had four or five boarders working for her who she cooked and did clothes washing for on top of her own family. Did the sewing and cleaning, canned enough vegetables to get through the winter, got everyone to church every Sunday, and she taught elementary school full time."

"Amazing," Charlie said. "Half the people I know talk about being stressed out just taking care of themselves."

The man gave Charlie a curious look, then went on. "If you ask me, Americans are the best workers in the world. There's nothing we can't do once we put our minds to it. Hell, we built the B-24 bomber; it has one million, five hundred and fifty thousand working parts, and at one Ford Motor Company plant they built one every sixty-three minutes for the last two years. We built a railroad that tied together two oceans. I wouldn't be surprised if someday we build spaceships that go to the moon. No, there's nothing we can't do. But half of it is just believing that you can do it. If that little girl believes in herself, she'll overcome the polio. She'll go on and do something great with her life. I'd bet on her if I was a betting man."

Charlie glanced at the window and when he saw that

their faces were gone he was filled again with the same lone-liness that had gripped him after the poker game ended.

"I'm going to quit for a while and eat all the food in the dining car," he heard one of the soldiers say. He drove his shovel into the snow and called to Charlie. "You coming?"

Charlie asked the man if his grandmother had ever been defeated by anything.

"Sure," he said. "Things got really hard during the Depression. All her kids sold potatoes for a penny apiece at the train station and outside the movie theater to get gas-oline money for the tractor. But she always said that God never gives people a heavier burden than they can carry. So, she had her faith. Plus she loved to dance. Whenever things got her down, she'd have my grandfather roll up the carpet in the living room and they'd dance. Waltz. Jitterbug. Fox Trot. You name it. They'd dance their sorrows away, I guess."

As they reached the iron steps of the locomotive, the soldier grabbed hold of the bronze railings and cleared all three steps in one graceful leap. "I sure hope I remem-ber how to dance again when I get the opportunity," he said.

Charlie had placed one foot on the bottom step to follow the man, but when he saw the drumming soldier walking alone alongside the tracks, his pint bottle of whis-key hanging down in one hand, and his head bowed, he followed him.

FIFTEEN

*T*hey ended up sitting out in the caboose, talking while a second wave of soldiers replaced the first and dug away at the mountain of snow.

"I heard the eastbound train will pull up alongside us soon," the soldier told Charlie. "So if you want to go back to New York City, that will be your chance."

"Sounds good," Charlie replied. But listening to the soldiers' stories and joining them in the shoveling had relieved him of the burden of thinking about himself, and now he felt relaxed, almost calm.

The soldier took off his green wool cap. "Look at this," he exclaimed. "Twenty-two years old and my hair is already turning white."

Before Charlie could say anything, the sound of the eastbound train's whistle flew across the sky.

"Must be our train," the soldier said. "Wind is out of the north today. I can feel the dampness in my knees. More snow coming, I'd say. It's funny, when I was a kid I spent all day outside every day, playing soldiers in the woods behind my house. Me and my buddies. The only bad part was when our mothers would call us home to eat and get to bed. In this man's army I spent two and a half years outside with nobody calling me in. Had five nights under a roof in all that time. Sure you don't want a drink?"

"No thanks," Charlie said.

"You're somebody I can talk to," the man said. "I'm going to miss that."

This surprised Charlie. "Well, thanks," he said.

"Something really bad happened in France," the man continued, his voice lower now, almost as if he were speaking to himself. "It was my first week in combat after Normandy. I was clearing a barn, looking for a German sniper. I was walking across the floor, staring up at this loft above me with my rifle zeroed in on it. I was taking baby steps, I knew someone was up there, I could feel it, you know? I heard a sound and then I saw something move and I pulled the trigger. Next thing I know, something fell on me from up there. I thought it was a sack of dirt or maybe potatoes. It was a little girl. She fell all the way down and landed right on top of me. Knocked me over in the hay. She was like a rag doll lying right across my face. It was like somebody had dropped her on me."

He paused for a moment and took another drink before he went on. "I never told anybody about this," he said.

"Well, I'm sorry," Charlie told him. "I mean, nobody should have to go through something like that. But it wasn't your fault. You have to remember that."

The sound of the eastbound train whistle reached them again, now sounding closer.

"You ready to jump ship?" the soldier asked Charlie.

"I have to go get my money," Charlie said.

It only took him a few moments, then he was back on the caboose with the sack of money over his shoulder.

"You look like Santa Claus," the soldier said with a smile.

They could hear the locomotive of the eastbound train now, growing nearer. "I spent some time last night with the nurse taking care of the wounded guys. She's from Brooklyn. She says after she's discharged she'll go back to Brooklyn and start a home for vets. So, how much poker money did you win, anyway?"

"Just enough to pay off some debts," Charlie said.

"Well, that's good, I guess," the man said to him.

"It's only the beginning," Charlie said, feeling the cold chill at his spine again. "I'll spend the rest of my life trying to dig myself out of a deep hole." Then he set the sack down in the snow and took the telegram from his pocket and held it in his hand, reading Sally's name.

"Bad news?" the soldier asked him.

"I guess so," Charlie said. "It's not for me. It's for this girl who got on the train with me in New York City."

"I've seen her," the man said. "Are you going to leave her behind?"

"Yeah," Charlie said slowly.

"What about the telegram?"

"I think I'll just pretend it never happened. Maybe none of this ever happened. Whatever's in this telegram, she's going to find out when she gets to California."

"Are you sure?"

"No, not really. I'm not really sure of too much right now."

"Who is?" the soldier asked. "Anyone who tells you he is, is a damned fool. The whole world is on its side now."

Charlie looked into the man's eyes and found wisdom and strength there.

The eastbound train appeared on the tracks beside them, its iron wheels squealing as it came to a stop. The soldier stood up and grabbed his duffle bag.

"Good luck," he said to Charlie. "I hope neither one of us ever has to fight in another war."

As they shook hands on the caboose, the man said, "It doesn't look like you'll be coming with me."

Charlie looked down at the telegram in his hand. "I guess not," he said.

The soldier nodded before he jumped down off the caboose into the snow.

"Is all this a dream?" Charlie called to him eagerly.

The man answered right away. "Well, I don't hear any shells exploding. And I don't see any dying boys crying out for their mothers. So, maybe it is a dream."

He hurried along the tracks, then climbed up on the caboose of the eastbound train, where he called back to Charlie. "You gave me some hope."

Charlie didn't quite hear what he'd said. "What was that?" he called back to him.

"I said, you gave me enough hope to go home." With that he unbuttoned his coat and took the dog tags from around his neck. "Here," he shouted. "Take these for good luck."

He tossed them through the air across the space between the two trains and Charlie caught them.

"Thanks," he called back. "I'll keep them." Just then, as the eastbound train began to pull away, the dog tags fell from Charlie's hand and he dropped down on his knees to pick them up. A gust of wind shook the telegram from his hand, and he had to dive for it so that it wouldn't blow away. When he had it safely back in his pocket, he bent down and began looking for the dog tags in the snow, but couldn't find them. He was still on his knees when he looked up and saw the eastbound train pulling away. The drumming soldier waved once to him before he went inside.

Charlie walked back to his room with his sack of money, passing through the car of wounded soldiers and feeling now, for a reason he couldn't understand, like he was one of them.

Back in his room he stood looking up at the empty beds. He was holding the Western Union telegram in one hand, reading Sally's name. When he raised his eyes to the window, he saw where his name was written in the frost in a child's hand. He stepped closer to the window and examined it, and saw where the child had forgotten the "h" and someone had inserted it, no doubt Sally. The letters were beginning to melt.

Charlie opened the telegram, then stood reading it:

I was wounded. . . You cannot come marry me.
Paul

*E*very table in the dining car was crowded with soldiers eating their breakfast. Sally and Scarlet were seated at a round table covered with a white linen cloth, closest to the kitchen, and Sally was pouring cream into her tea when Charlie's voice rose above the conversation and the singing. He was standing just inside the door at the far end of the car, and the moment he saw her through the tables of soldiers, he called out to her in a voice that was loud enough to silence everyone. As soon as he said her name, she turned towards him, staring at his face as he went on, "Most of us miss the real story of our lives." The car fell silent and everyone turned in their seats to regard him. He waited for Sally to call back, "What real story?"

"The story we were put in this world to live," he answered. He saw her lean down and lift the child up in her arms.

"Why do we miss it?" she called back.

"Because it doesn't belong to us. It's someone else's story. We're just a part of it."

They were not his words, they were hers, but he felt their purpose with an absolute conviction as he watched her and the child looking at him. He saw that they were waiting for the next thing he would say to fill the silence, and he wanted to say more; he wanted to say that the world was no longer round, but flat, and that this train they were traveling on would never arrive anywhere, and that he was the one person on earth they could depend on. He wanted to tell them something that would make a difference in the hours and days ahead, when they were going to cross that space that separates how we dream our lives will turn out, and how they do.

But he said nothing more. He walked back to his room and was standing at the window, looking down at the telegram in his hands in a narrow blade of sunlight, when Sally came up behind him. Before he turned, he slid the telegram back into his pocket.

"Maurice has Scarlet helping with the dishes," she said, then turned away shyly.

Charlie took note of her shyness and it gave him confidence. "What do you know about the past?" he asked her.

She looked confused. "The past?" she asked.

"Does it become the future, or is it just left behind?"

"I don't know," she said. "Maybe it depends on what we choose to remember."

He took a half step closer to her and waited until she was looking into his eyes. "I remember you from before," he said.

"When?" she asked.

"In New York City."

"I've spent time there the last three years," she said.

"Where do you live?" he asked her.

"I've been in Connecticut, living at the orphanage where I work. Do you live in the city?"

He told her that he did. "I remember you from a little shop on 57th Street, off Fifth Avenue, where you bought a dress for your flower girl."

He gestured to the eight-sided box on the chair.

"You were there?" she said.

"I was."

"The store was crowded, and I wasn't paying attention to the other people," she said.

"Your fiancé's name is Paul. Before the war, the two of you moved to New York because of Walt Whitman. Paul writes poetry and Whitman is his favorite poet."

When he saw her confusion, he wanted to make it easier and so he added, "I heard you telling the woman who sold you the dress for your flower girl."

She seemed relieved. "Yes," she said, "a lovely man and his wife. They had emigrated from a small village in Italy."

"Your wedding is on Christmas day?" he asked.

"Yes, in three days," she said.

He turned away and looked out the window at a field of fir trees lined up in rows like soldiers in formation.

"I think I'd better check on Scarlet," she said. "That

was a lovely thing you said about us being a part of someone else's story. It's so much like something my Paul would say."

She stepped through the doorway, out into the corridor, and told him that she would see him again.

"Yes," he said.

After she left, Charlie took his sack of money from beneath the lower berth and walked back to the car with the wounded soldiers. He asked the nurse to find a pen and paper and then he sat beside her. "If you live in Brooklyn, why are you going to California?" he asked her.

"My orders are to accompany these soldiers to San Francisco," she told him. "I'll be discharged there, then head home."

"And what are you going to do back in Brooklyn?"

"I'll work as a nurse until I save enough money to open up a place for vets. A little boarding house or something, anything is better than a hospital. There will be boys in New York who are going to need to be cared for, for the rest of their lives."

"I suppose you're right," Charlie told her. "What's your name?"

"Lieutenant Kelly," she said. "Martha Kelly."

"Well, Lieutenant, today is your lucky day." He gave her the money and told her to write down his instructions. "There's going to be a stock that comes onto the market named Xerox. I want you to spend all of this money on it. Buy as many shares as you can, and hold them for twenty-two years. Then I want you to sell one hundred shares and buy a stock called Sun Computers. Nine years later, I want you to sell three hundred shares and spend all of that on a stock called Apple. Are you writing all this down?"

"Yes," she told him, "but I don't know a thing about the stock market."

"Don't worry. I'm telling you everything you'll ever need to know. Trust me. If you do these things, you'll have plenty of money to take care of as many veterans as you want. You'll have plenty for yourself, too. Do you want to have kids?"

"Yes, I hope to," she said.

"Well," Charlie told her, "they'll never have to worry about money, either."

"That's really wonderful," she said.

"That's America," he told her.

SEVENTEEN

*I*t was a long night for Charlie as the train made its way into Manitoba. He spent the hours sitting in the bar and walking the length of the train, which he now knew was seventeen cars, including a baggage car, where he'd found a piano. In the first light of a new morning, he stood in the doorway of his room, looking in at Sally and Scarlet as they slept. It was cold enough in the room to see his breath and theirs and to set him into motion, taking the blankets from his bed again to cover them, then spreading their coats over them as well. He lingered for a moment, gazing at their faces. And just as he began to turn away, the child opened her eyes and asked him if he would carry her to the toilet. "I don't want to wake Sally," she said.

Charlie opened the door to the bathroom and a pale light went on overhead. When he looked back, she was reaching to him with outstretched arms, waiting for him to lift her from the bed, which he did self-consciously as if he were carrying a fragile parcel that might break in his hands. "How long have you known Sally?" he asked her.

"Oh, a very long time," she said.

"And you live in New York City with her?"

"Nope. We live in Connecticut, in the orphanage. But my dress is from New York City. That's where Sally went to buy it. You should see how pretty it is, Charlie."

Before he could ask her his next question, she put one of her own to him. "So, do you think Paul will be a good husband to Sally? I mean, will he stay with her forever and ever? Because if they don't stay together, she's going to be really sad. You can close the door now and I'll call you when I'm finished."

Her question left him practically breathless, and he leaned against the door with his eyes closed and a soft pounding at the back of his head. Then she called his name again. "Yeah," he managed to say.

"I don't think you're a real farmer," she said.

"You don't?"

"Because your hands are too soft. Don't farmers' hands get all worn out from the work?"

"I really don't know," he said.

"Well, even if you're not a real farmer, you're still real, aren't you, Charlie?"

He thought about this, then said, "I guess that's the question."

A moment later she called to him, "I'm finished. You can get me now."

After he had carried her back to the bed, she told him that Sally had taught her how to salute like a soldier, and to prove it, she saluted him.

"Very good," he said. "And you were waiting for her in Connecticut, right?"

"I already told you, Charlie," she said. "At the orphanage. She had to go into the city first to get my dress." She pulled a book out from under her pillow and asked if she could read to him.

"Isn't it too dark for you to see the words?" he asked.

"I remember all the words," she said.

"What's it called?"

"*The Little Prince*."

"I don't know that story."

"Sure you do," she assured him. "You probably just forgot." Then she began reciting from memory: "Once, when I was six years old, I saw a magnificent picture in a book called 'True Stories from Nature.' It was a picture of a boa constrictor. I can't show you the drawing because it's too dark."

Just then Sally turned in her sleep so that Charlie could see her face. He was close enough to feel her breath on his skin. He thought again of the telegram and how terribly her life was going to change. Not only her life, but the child's life as well.

"What's wrong, Charlie?" he heard Scarlet saying. "You look scared."

"I have to go now," he replied as he hurried from the room.

EIGHTEEN

*A*s Charlie passed through each open vestibule on his way to the dining car, he felt like he was moving in the wrong direction and that he might never be able to turn around again and cross the space between him and Sally that widened with each step he took.

The dining car was empty. The morning light lay across the bare tables and his shoes, as he counted his echoing footsteps while he walked to the kitchen door. When he pushed it open, he was astonished to see the drumming soldier wrapped in blankets, moving about the kitchen quickly. When the man looked up and saw Charlie standing there, he took his appearance in stride, as if he had always believed they would see each other again. "Maurice must still be sleeping," he said. "I decided I wanted to get something to eat, but everything is frozen hard as concrete."

With this, he picked up an egg and tossed it against the refrigerator, where it hit with a thud, fell to the floor like a rock, and rolled under a table. "You see what I'm up against?" he exclaimed.

Finally Charlie shook off his surprise and spoke. "You got off the train," he said. "Is this another trick?"

"No trick, " he replied. "I got off the train and then I got back on."

"Why?"

"I thought maybe I could be of some help to you with this girl problem you've got," he said.

"You threw me your dog tags, but I lost them in the snow," Charlie said as he leaned against one of the cook-stoves. "I'm sorry."

"Not a problem," the soldier said. "I don't need them anymore."

He took a long look at Charlie and his expression turned to deep concern. "You don't look well, mister," he said, "and unfortunately for both of us, I'm out of whiskey until the bar opens again. Dry as a bone, I'm afraid."

"That's alright," Charlie replied. He took the telegram from his pocket. Without saying anything, he handed it to him.

"Oh, right, the telegram," the soldier said gravely. He took it reluctantly and walked to a window, where he opened and read it. When he had finished, he folded it neatly, placed it inside the envelope, and gazed out the window. "That's tough," he said.

"Yeah," Charlie said. "What should I do?"

The silence that followed unsettled him. The soldier

was still standing at the window, but his head was bowed and he looked like he might have fallen asleep.

When Charlie took a step toward him, he didn't move. "Excuse me," he said. "Excuse me." Then, just as Charlie was reaching for him, to touch his shoulder, the man spang to life.

"When I was a kid, I took this long train ride with my great aunt, Doris," he said. "It was during the Depression, and she was traveling to New Mexico to ask another relative for money. I guess the family figured if they took a kid along, it would cover the sympathy angle or something, I don't know. Anyway, there was nothing to do on the train for three days except look out the windows, and she told me that if you ride the train long enough, you see in the distance every important time in your life. The day when you first rode a bicycle. The night you first kissed a girl. The day you lost somebody you loved."

He paused for a moment and held the telegram in his outstretched hand. Charlie walked to his side and took it. For another few seconds, before the soldier went on, both men stood there watching the rising light of morning. " 'All those moments are out there,' she said," he continued. "They are being lived by someone else the same way we lived them. All we have to do is watch from the window of a train. And so, if you ride this train long enough, maybe you'll see somebody like yourself searching for an answer, and for the right words, I suppose."

"Words?" Charlie asked.

"The words to tell this gal and her child."

"What words could possibly make it any easier for them?"

He seemed to have an answer. "You can't make it easier, that's true. But maybe you can find a way to let them know that life will go on without this wounded soldier, who doesn't want them anymore. The sun will rise again tomorrow like it does every morning."

"That doesn't help," Charlie said grimly.

The soldier shook his head thoughtfully and said, "I think this guy must love her truly, if you ask me."

Charlie disagreed. "To send her this? He can't be thinking about anyone but himself and what he wants."

The soldier looked into his eyes. "You could be right," he said. "But what would you do if it was you? For me, the worst thing would be to become a burden on the person I love. That was the one thing I prayed for in this rotten war. I couldn't stand the idea that I could ever be a burden on anyone."

Now Charlie was confused. He hadn't thought of it that way. "I can't do this," he told the soldier. "It's not my job to tell her anything, or try to make her see anything."

"Maybe you can just be there to listen, then," he said with great sincerity.

Charlie looked at him as he nodded his head slowly to encourage him. "Think about it," he said.

Then old Maurice came bounding into the kitchen with a robe draped over his shoulders that fell to the floor. He was waving his arms and muttering to himself. "Overslept again!" he exclaimed. "In one hour I will ask to stop the train at the Cathance River. It is the only river that moves rapidly enough not to freeze. We must catch some fish to feed our passengers. Do you fish, messieurs?"

"Not me, sorry," the soldier said, throwing up his hands for emphasis.

Both men turned to Charlie.

"Sure," Charlie said.

NINETEEN

*I*t had begun to snow again by the time the train stopped, and Charlie, wearing the only pair of snow-shoes on board and carrying a fishing rod, made his way down the tracks. "How many people are we feeding?" he called back to Maurice.

"Too many, Charlie," he answered. "An army! Think of the Bible, my young friend. The miracle of the loaves and fishes."

As Charlie made his way toward a clearing, he glanced back at the train and saw Sally and Scarlet at their window, watching him. He waved once and when he saw the child's hand go up at the window, he turned back and began walking toward them with his head raised so that he never took his eyes off them. At the window he said to Scarlet, "Do you have warm clothes?"

Her eyes lit up when she realized that he was inviting her along, and a few moments later she rode on Charlie's shoulders through a cathedral of silence, a world of snow-capped hills and dark green, pointed fir trees.

At the river bank Charlie cast the line, then placed the rod in her hands. "I once fished the Amazon for parakeet trout," he told her. "Did you already know that?"

She was puzzled by his question. "How would I know that?" she asked.

"Oh," he said, "I just thought I might be repeating myself, that's all. Anyway, that's the only place on earth where you can catch them. They fly, you know?"

"Fish that fly? I like that. Hey, Charlie, what if these fish don't like frozen hot dogs?"

"I was thinking the same thing," Charlie said. These words were barely out of his mouth when the rod bent mightily and the child had a fish on the line. They brought it in slowly together, a big beautiful rainbow trout whose belly was iridescent in the bright daylight. Charlie took it off the hook and after one more cast Scarlet caught another fish. And then another. It went on like this until their astonishment gave way and they were just two people fishing and talking in Canada. When she asked him if he had ever been to California and he told her that he had a few times, she said, "But you never sailed a boat in the stars there, I bet."

"You're right, I never have done that."

"Well, maybe you should come with us."

"Oh, I don't know anyone there."

"You know us."

"Yes, now I know you, that's true."

"How many more fish do you want me to catch, Charlie? We already have sixteen."

"As many as we can," he said.

They had twice that many when they made their way back along the river to the train. "What kind of kid were you?" she wanted to know.

"I don't know, really," he said.

"You mean you forgot?"

"No, no, I still remember. I was just like you."

"You mean crippled like me?"

"Your legs don't work like mine do, but my imagination doesn't work like yours."

"I don't understand."

"Well, when you read your book about the little prince, do you understand it?"

"Of course, every word."

"Well then, see? I don't, because my imagination isn't strong like yours."

"Maybe it will get stronger. And maybe I'll be able to stand up someday, like President Roosevelt did before he died."

"I bet you will," he told her. "I bet that someday your legs will be as good as new."

A moment later there was only the sound of their laughter rising above the rushing river. Behind them there was the pale shadow of the moon rising over an empty field where the new snow lay evenly.

TWENTY

*L*ater that day, Scarlet sat on the counter in the kitchen reading her *Little Prince* to Maurice while he prepared the fish. And in the open vestibule where Charlie had stood with the drumming soldier, he now stood talking with Sally while the country passed by. "Is it this beautiful on your farm?" she asked him.

He was looking right into her eyes when he answered, "No, not this beautiful."

She knew he meant her, and she looked away demurely.

He told her then that the beauty of the world was lost on him. "I can't name a bird or a constellation in the night sky. I'm a modern man, Sally. I work too hard to notice the beauty."

"Being a hard worker is a virtue," she reminded him.

"Not in my case. I work because I'm afraid to fail. I want to win."

"What is it that you want to win, Charlie?" she asked.

He shrugged and thought about her question, wanting to answer honestly. "I just want to win so much that I won't have to ever be afraid of losing again. What about you? What are you afraid of, Sally?"

She seemed startled, and asked him to say her name again. He didn't understand, but he obliged. "Sally," he said.

"For a second, your voice reminded me of someone else," she said.

"Who?" he asked.

"I don't know, really. I'm sorry."

Charlie waited, hoping she might say more, but when she didn't, he told her that he needed to talk with her about something.

"What is it?" she asked.

"After lunch," he said.

In the dining car, Sally and Maurice and Charlie, with Scarlet riding on his shoulders, served the soldiers their fresh trout. Each time Charlie looked at Sally, he was filled with a sense of dread.

"What do you want from Santa?" one soldier asked the child.

"My own fishing rod," she said.

This brought a smile to Charlie's face.

Another soldier asked Sally if she would kiss him. "Just one time," he asked.

"Strictly prohibited," she said with a smile.

"Prohibited by who?" the soldier asked. "I want to meet that sourpuss. I'm afraid that I might have forgotten how to do it."

Sally touched his face tenderly and said, "When you get home there will be girls for you to kiss who will remind you how to do it. But I'll sing for you if you'd like."

"Hey, I'll take what I can get," he said.

They began singing 'Silent Night.' Maurice sang in French. At first it was just another Christmas carol, but gradually, as each soldier receded into his own private thoughts and memories, a deeply contemplative mood settled over the train that neither the soldiers nor Charlie would ever forget. It was as if their singing had transformed the train into a sanctuary of prayers. They were singing the second verse when the train slowed to a crawl as they passed through a village. Just before the train began to pick up speed again, Charlie saw the drumming soldier standing at the side of the tracks with his duffle bag over his shoulder. He hurried to a window and called out to him, "Hey, hey?" But the soldier didn't hear him. By now, others in the dining car were trying to help Charlie get the man's attention, calling to the soldier, and one man was trying to open a window. Charlie pushed on the window with him, but it wouldn't budge. Finally he ran out of the car into the next vestibule. He managed to unlatch the door and push it open, but the moment he called to the soldier again, the train whistle drowned his voice and all Charlie could do was watch him disappear into the station as the train pulled away.

When they had finished lunch, while Sally and Scarlet helped Maurice clean up the dishes, Charlie went to the locomotive's boiler room to shovel coal with three soldiers. They worked shirtless and were soon covered in sweat and black dust. When they spoke they had to shout to hear one another above the clamoring engine. For a while Charlie was lost in his own thoughts of the drumming soldier who was gone now. Charlie would never know his name or where he was going. That feeling of deep loneliness ran through him again.

"A farm in Alberta? That sounds good to me," one soldier said after some time had passed.

"Not bad," Charlie replied. "Where are you headed?"

"San Francisco, by way of Vancouver, now, I guess. I figure that I'll find a nice noisy bar that stays open late every night of the week."

Another soldier chimed in. "I'll be driving my cab in San Jose again soon. I was taking a fare to Milt Durocher's Barber Shop when it came over the radio that Pearl Harbor had been bombed by the Japs. I dropped the fare, then went straight to the recruiting center at my old high school and enlisted in the infantry."

"You boys ever wonder what the world is going to be like in another fifty, sixty years?" Charlie asked them.

"Before the war, maybe," one answered him. "But not anymore."

"Me neither," another said. "I just hope people stop hating each other so much."

"What is it like to be as old as you are?" the first soldier asked Charlie.

"How old do you think I am, anyway?" Charlie asked.

"Thirty?"

"Thirty-two actually," Charlie told them. "When I was your age, I started working seventy hours a week. By the time I got to age twenty-five, I was working ninety-five hours a week. So, you've got that to look forward to."

"That's what I fought the friggin war for, so I could work myself to death?" one man said. "I'll tell you, if there's one thing this war taught me, it's that now that it's over, I'm going to have some fun. I'm going to spend a lot of time having fun."

"Good for you," Charlie said. "Tell me something— how do you have fun? I mean, how does a person have fun?

"Are you nuts?" the third man said. "You don't know how to have fun? I guess you've been on the farm too long, pal."

"I'm serious," Charlie said. "It's an art that I never learned."

"Spend a couple days with me and I'll teach you!" the soldier next to him said.

They all had a good laugh and for a moment Charlie forgot all about the telegram in his pocket. "The world has changed a lot while you boys were gone," he said. "It's tough, and it's going to get a lot tougher. And I'll tell you what you're going to miss about the war. This. This right here. Time for friends to spend together. It's hard to hold on to friends out there now. And as for progress, well, someday men will walk on the moon, and we'll use telephones without cords that you can carry in your shirt pocket, but we'll never stop hating each other. There will always be more war."

Everyone was silent for a moment. Finally one soldier said, "You can have the telephones and the moon. All I want is a girl like yours. If I can find a girl like yours, I won't care about anything else."

"I need to ask you guys something," Charlie said solemnly. "If you'd been wounded in the war, would you tell your girl that she couldn't marry you?"

The soldiers thought about this while they worked in silence. Finally one of them said, "If I'd got it bad, yeah, I wouldn't want to drag her through it."

"Same here," said another man. "But I don't know for sure."

The third man was certain, he said. "I wouldn't ask nobody to live half a life for me," he said. "Not if I loved her."

Charlie looked at him, stunned by his conviction. He was going to say more, but he let it go.

TWENTY-ONE

*C*harlie found Sally cutting her hair in their room, while Scarlet took a nap. She was concentrating hard when his reflection appeared beside hers in the glass. She gazed at his face for a moment as if he were someone she had grown comfortable with, like an old friend who had casually come calling.

She continued cutting her hair, and told him that it had grown so long since the last time she and Paul were together, that she was afraid he might not recognize her. Sadness swept across her eyes.

"You're going to be married on Christmas day," Charlie said.

She lowered her hands, regarding his face in the mirror. "I told you?"

"You did."

"I don't remember telling you," she said.

"Maybe I dreamed it," Charlie said.

"You've been dreaming about me?" she asked.

"I guess I have."

"In two days," she said, "you'll be back on your farm in Alberta and it will be my wedding day."

He nodded, then said, "Well, short hair or long, I'm sure he hasn't forgotten how you look. And if you're a few days late, it will be worth his wait." He gestured toward Scarlet and went on. "And just wait until he sees your flower girl. He won't be able to resist either of you."

Sally told him that she and her fiancé were going to adopt her. And then a weariness seemed to come over her. Her eyes closed and she began to sway. "I think it's just that I'm anxious," she told him. "I've been waiting for my real life to begin, and now that it's here, I'm—" She stopped suddenly.

"What?" he asked her.

"The waiting has been hard for me. Wishing away the days and weeks. I'm not as good at it as some people seem to be. I've told myself that for as long as I live, I'm never again going to wish time away, once I'm with Paul. We're not going to waste a day."

Just then two soldiers, swaying arm in arm after a little too much to drink, passed the room singing at the top of their lungs, "Glory, Glory, what a hell of a way to die!"

"They're all just kids, and they've already done more in their lives than I'll ever do," Charlie said.

"You can't say that," Sally told him. "You have no idea what lies ahead."

He thought about this, then said, "I'm afraid I do."

"If you can see into the future, will you tell me how many children Paul and I are going to have?"

He just gave her a little smile. "No, don't tell me," she said. "I want it to be a surprise, but tell me, please, does my hair look terrible now?"

"Not at all," he said. "It will grow back anyway," he said.

"Ah, you're looking into the future again," she joked. It was her smile that made him decide this was the right time.

"I have something to show you," he said.

He took the telegram from his pocket.

Her hand fell on his arm as she said, "Oh Charlie, please don't tell me that you've lost someone."

He looked toward Scarlet first to make sure she was still sleeping, then his eyes met Sally's as he told her, "It's for you. I shouldn't have opened it."

She was reluctant to take it from his hand. "I don't understand," she said. Then she read it slowly, folded it and put it back inside the envelope. She took it out a moment later and read it a second time. When she looked up at him, it all came pouring out of him. "In the store you tried on a wedding dress and for a moment I felt sure of something," he began. "I haven't felt that way in a long time, Sally. I don't think this will make any sense to you, or help you in any way, but I got on this train to be with you. And when this telegram arrived, I started to believe that I could take Paul's place. I even thought of telling you that he'd been killed so that I could have you. And so you wouldn't be caught in the middle like this, not knowing what to do."

He paused long enough to see that she was breaking into little pieces in front of him. "It's not fair," she whispered.

He wanted to reach for her hand but he didn't dare. "Maybe it's not real, Sally," he said.

She didn't hear this.

"Whatever has happened to Paul," she said, "no matter how bad it is, how could he expect that I would just start my life again without even seeing him? As a man, can you answer that question for me?"

Charlie felt as helpless as a child. He just stood there, shaking his head slowly.

"This war has gone on and on," she said, "and there are so many casualties. Even now, when the war is over, still peoples' lives are being destroyed by it. I think it has eaten my life out of me."

She turned away as if Charlie weren't there. He watched her climb up into the bunk and take her place beside Scarlet. He didn't know what to do or say. He glanced out the window. The train had slowed again and he saw three soldiers jump off and quickly cut down a small evergreen tree and haul it onto the train. When he looked back at Sally, she had closed her eyes. He stood there for a while, wondering what was real and how it was going to end. He remembered how he'd felt on those days with the company, when he walked out into the evening after making more money in thirteen hours than most people made in ten years of work. He had wondered then if that was real. If he were real. In a way, he had known that it couldn't be real. It was just something that was happening as a result of a random coalescing of molecules. Now, gazing at Sally and Scarlet, they seemed more substantial than that. He reached out and placed his hand on the child's hand. He saw her eyelids flutter.

TWENTY-TWO

*A*s darkness fell and the train barreled across Manitoba and into Saskatchewan, Maurice and Charlie sat listening to Scarlet read in the kitchen. Nurse Kelly helped a wounded soldier from Detroit write a letter to the pastor of his church, and Sally slept in the upper berth in Charlie's room, where she had spent most of the day. Eventually Charlie carried the child to his room so she could join her, and then he spent the night drinking coffee alone in the dining car.

That is where Sally found him, just before the first light of dawn. She entered the car from the far end and when he turned, she was walking toward him. "My father always knew what to say to me whenever I was confused," she said as she sat down next to Charlie. "He's a simple man. He works for Sears and Roebuck. Do you know that soon you'll be able to order almost anything from their catalog? Even a house. Everything will be shipped by truck right to your door. Including plumbing pipes, electrical wire, windows. Even bricks for your fireplace and chimney. All the soldiers coming home will need houses."

When she stopped, Charlie said, "I guess that's true."

She stared into his eyes for a moment as if she were remembering who he was. Then she said, "This is a terrible thing to think, but in my love story with Paul, I was never sure that he loved me as much as I loved him. It's almost never equal, is it? And after I read the telegram, I thought, well, now Paul will need me the way that I have needed him. And I've always thought that the place where we are broken is the place where another person gets to become part of our life. That's what I have always believed. But now I don't know what to think."

Her expression changed and she narrowed her eyes.

"Isn't there supposed to be a progression in our lives?" she said. "First we wait for love, and after we find it, we wait for the changes that love will bring. I believed in this when I promised Scarlet that she would be our flower girl, and that after Paul and I were married, we would adopt her. How can I tell her that we are no longer wanted? She's never been wanted before. Who wants a child with polio? You see? But nothing about this is right anymore. I did what I was supposed to do. For three years I remained true to Paul. I got down on my knees every morning and again each night, and I prayed for him. I waited and I wrote my heart out in letters. I kept my vigil, Charlie."

Until she spoke his name, he wasn't sure she even knew that he was there beside her. When she spoke again, a softness had returned to her voice that fell slowly, like a piece of paper riding the wind. "I keep telling myself that whatever happened to Paul to make him change his mind, when he sees me again . . . well, is this stupid of me?"

"No," Charlie said emphatically. "No, it's not stupid. I think you're right. I really do."

She rose to her feet then, and after thanking him, walked away and left him there.

He spent a long day walking from car to car, and helping Maurice prepare meals for the soldiers. That night, Charlie told Sally and Scarlet that some of the soldiers had decorated a tree and were going to have a little party in the baggage car, where there was a piano that was being shipped to the West Coast.

He didn't expect them to come, but they did. And they both took turns dancing with the soldiers, Scarlet being passed around like a rag doll. Charlie watched from the shadows, rehearsing what he was going to say to Sally when he asked her to dance with him. He couldn't stop wanting her for his own, and when she was in his arms he whispered into her ear, "I want you to come with me back to New York. We'll start a new life there together. You and Scarlet and I. No more sorrow. A good life, I promise you." He felt her body against his and though she said nothing, he believed that he could reach her and that if he said the right things, he might hold her this close forever. "We'll go back to the little shop and get you the wedding dress that you tried on, Sally. We'll stay in the Waldorf Hotel."

She leaned away and stepped out of his embrace. In her eyes there was a cold and troubling apprehension that made Charlie regret everything he'd said. He began to apologize, but she was already walking away. He watched her take Scarlet into her arms. She turned back and said, "In my sleep I am already in California. Paul and I are married."

She stood still for a moment looking back at him, and he wondered if his life had become an impenetrable web of dreams. Maybe he had died, he thought, and this was his next life. He found himself wanting some deep and meaningful explanation for how he felt. What was happening was totally different from anything he'd experienced before. This was a completely new dimension of time; it was time with physical properties of heat and light and such blinding intensity that it was as if they'd known each other in past worlds and had waited across lifetimes for the present to draw them back together. But he could tell now that she was receding from his world. He knew that by the hollow sound of her voice and the ghostly, crooked smile she managed to show him. When the piano stopped, her eyes began to flash about restlessly, searching for a way out, and he watched the soldiers step aside and let her pass.

TWENTY-THREE

*H*ours later, in the dead of the night, Charlie sat in the bar with a few soldiers, passing his lifeless iPhone around for them to look at. They stared at it as if it had fallen from some other galaxy. They had all had too much to drink. "You say you made this?" one soldier asked.

"Not me," Charlie said. "Some guy in California, I think."

"And it's a telephone?"

"Yep. When it's working it is. And it's got music on it. And here's a camera right here."

"I'd like to have one of these, if you ever figure out how to make it work."

"You will," Charlie told him. "You'll be an old man by then, but you will."

The soldiers looked incredulous as Charlie put the thing in his pocket and ordered another drink.

Just then Maurice burst into the car and called his name.

"You must hurry, Charlie," he said. "The child is very sick."

When they reached the room they found Sally holding Scarlet tightly against her, as Nurse Kelly finished taking her temperature.

"It's one hundred and five now," she said with great concern.

Charlie left them and went running the length of the train, until he reached the locomotive where the engineer was driving with his face pressed to the windshield, trying to see through the blowing snow. "When do we pass the next town with a hospital?" Charlie questioned him.

"Melville," he said. He checked his watch. "Two hours at this speed. But the hospital is miles from the station."

"I'll need to get off with a sick child."

They were ready when the train stopped. Charlie in his overcoat and snowshoes. Sally with Scarlet in her arms, wrapped in blankets. And Maurice, who gestured to the window where a scatter of lights appeared through the trees. "Melville," he said.

Charlie jumped down into the snow, and Sally passed the child to him. He had a sense that he had been blind all his life. Blind to the grief others suffered and the pain they endured. He had placed himself at the center of every hour he had lived. He had been healthy every day of his life. He had never been in danger. He had been loved and protected and somehow he had become a man who never acknowledged how lucky he was. "It'll be alright," he said to Sally. And then he began running. Other soldiers gathered at the open door and watched until Charlie had disappeared over the hill.

He ran through the freezing-cold air and the blowing snow and the burning in his lungs without a thought of not reaching the hospital in time. Once, he became disoriented and when he looked down in the snow he saw the prints of his snowshoes and knew that he had somehow turned around. For a while, the lights that he was running towards disappeared as he weaved his way through the trees. When he felt himself tiring, he thought about the soldiers on the train who had been through experiences far more difficult than this. He thought of the wounded boys who would never be able to run anywhere again and he ran even harder.

He sat on her bed all night at the little hospital, which was nothing more than a boarding house with fireplaces in every room and a ship's clock in the foyer that struck a bell with the arrival of each new hour. When Scarlet opened her eyes at dawn, Charlie could tell that her fever had broken. He smiled at her and she smiled back. He told her where she was and she said that she remembered running through the woods. "All night while I waited here, I thought about my father," he told her. "And I realized something. Something that I should have realized a long time ago. I want to tell you. And I know that you will always remember."

"Okay," she said, listening intently.

"Most of the time when people disappoint us in this life, they're really just doing the best that they can. They don't mean to hurt us. We just expect too much."

When he finished she said, "There are tears coming from your eyes, Charlie."

"Really?" he said. "I'm just happy to see you feeling better." He hugged her and began to wonder what it would be like to know someone well. To wake each morning beside people you loved. To know the weight of someone's hand against your palm. He held the child for a long time. With one hand she reached to the window and wrote his name in the frost as she had on the train. By now there was barely a world left around them except for this world.

TWENTY-FOUR

*T*hey returned to the train and to a hero's welcome, soldiers crowded at the windows and in all the open vestibules, cheering as they approached. Charlie handed Scarlet to Sally, who had tears running down her cheeks. Maurice shook his hand and said softly, "Tonight, Charlie."

"Tonight?" Charlie said.

"Yes, this night is your night, my young farmer friend."

After darkness had fallen, Maurice said to Charlie, "You want her, I can see this in your eyes. So why don't you try?"

It took Charlie off guard. "Try what, Maurice?"

"Try tonight to claim her for your own."

"What about the soldier she is engaged to?" Charlie asked him.

"Don't ask me about him," Maurice said. He had polished the stainless steel bottom of a cooking pot, and was holding it for a mirror while Charlie shaved. "Ah, monsieur," he exclaimed, "you are already looking like a prince."

As Charlie finished, Maurice produced a bottle of wine. "And this as well, my friend," he said. "This is a 1912 Rothschild from a cellar in Paris." He blew the dust off the bottle.

"Are you sure?" Charlie finally asked him.

Maurice gave him a long look. "Yes, of course I am sure. I will open this bottle tonight to celebrate the end of war and the beginning of love. How could there be a better occasion? It is your occasion, monsieur. After the little one is fast asleep, I want you and Sally to come here and share this wine."

"Will you join us?" Charlie asked.

"*Non monsieur*, I will certainly not join you. But you must promise me that you will tell her what is in your heart."

Now Charlie finally understood. "You're trying to protect her," he said.

"Both of you," Maurice corrected him. "It is the responsibility of the old to protect the young."

"You don't think she should go to California?"

"I don't know," he said. "I am like her. I cannot decide. I am thinking, a man broken into pieces, does he not deserve to be loved just as anyone else? And how he must love her to tell her not to come, because he does not want to be a burden to her. That kind of love is very rare in the world, Charlie. In fact, I have thought that it was gone from the world completely. But then I think, here are you now, a farmer from Alberta, and I see the way you look at her and the way she looks at you, and I think you should take them off this train with you before it reaches the Pacific Ocean."

It hit Charlie how deceitful he had been with everyone on this train. It made him turn away with shame.

"There is something that you won't tell me, monsieur?" Maurice said.

Charlie took a deep breath, unsure what he would say next. "I'm not who you think I am, Maurice," he began. "I have no kind of life to give them."

Maurice waited, then nodded slowly as he said, "I see."

Some time passed before he said, "You don't give someone a life, Charlie; you build that life with them."

Charlie was lost in his own thoughts. "There are things I'm always going to remember," he said softly. "The way she looks out the window of the train. The sound of the little girl's voice first thing in the morning. The light in her hair. I can't imagine never seeing them again. I'm sorry. I don't even know what I am talking about."

"You love them, monsieur," Maurice said.

Charlie looked into his eyes and replied, "Yes, I guess I do."

This seemed to reassure the old man. He smiled knowingly and said, "That is all that matters. Love is all you ever really need in this world, Charlie."

He saw the doubt in Charlie's eyes. "You do not believe this?" he asked.

"I wish it were true, Maurice," Charlie said.

Maurice pressed him. "What makes you say that? You wish it were true?"

"I don't know Maurice. It just seems to me that people need a lot more than love."

"For example?"

"Well, money."

"Paper? It is only the external. I am speaking, *mon ami*, about the internal. Love that feeds you inside. If I said that you and Sally and the child could live the rest of your lives on this train, would you need anything else to be happy? Or would their love be enough for you?"

Charlie didn't have to think about this. "I wouldn't need anything else," he replied.

Maurice smiled. "Your world circumscribed by her touch. And hers by yours. That is my definition of love."

A little while later Charlie stood in the threshold of their room, watching Sally put Scarlet to bed for the night. "I was wondering if anybody ever wanted me, Sally?" he heard her ask.

Sally answered right away. "Of course," she told her. "A lot of people who came to the orphanage wanted you. But we wouldn't let you go unless they were just the right people. I've told you that before."

"I know," Scarlet said, "but I was just wondering—the people who wanted me, what were they like?"

"Well, they were nice, but they weren't ready to have children."

"Why not?"

"A lot of people who are nice aren't ready because they haven't learned to see things the way the Little Prince does."

"With their hearts, you mean?"

"Exactly. You shouldn't have children until you learn to see with your heart. Right?"

"And you and I are going to teach Paul, right? And after the wedding I will get to call you Mommy?"

Sally turned slightly and from where Charlie was standing, he could see that she was breaking into pieces inside.

"That's right," she said.

"You can go now," Scarlet told her. "I can fall asleep by myself."

Sally kissed her goodnight.

"You can kiss me, too, if you want, Charlie," the child called to him.

He walked over to her, saying, "I didn't think you could see me standing there."

"I saw you," she said.

And so he kissed her and she thanked him and gave him her soldier's salute again. "We'll be back soon," he told her.

TWENTY-FIVE

*T*hey stepped onto the little porch at the back of the caboose that Maurice had prepared like a sidewalk cafe in Paris. Two chairs with blankets. A table under a white, starched linen cloth. And a coal fire burning in a big soup pot to keep them warm. The bottle of wine was chilling in a bucket of snow, and as soon as they settled beneath the blankets and looked up, in the sky above them were the northern lights.

"It's magic," Sally commented as she sat down. "I'm sorry that I got so upset."

"No, please," Charlie said to her. "You don't need to be sorry about anything. I frightened you. I'm the one who's sorry."

She looked into his eyes. "When were you most happy in your life, Charlie?" she asked.

He answered right away in complete honesty. "Here with you," he said.

"Are you sure?"

"Yes, I'm sure," he said.

"And when were you least happy?"

"Here with you," he said again. "Because I know that our time together is running out."

She looked away, then back into his eyes. "Our time is always running out, Charlie," she said. "This night is going to end. It's what we make of it that counts. Most people waste so much time." She took his hand then, and asked him what he wanted most in this world.

"I want you and Scarlet," he said. And this answer seemed to him the most natural thing.

"And what else?" she asked.

"Nothing. I don't care about anything else," he said.

"But you did before?"

"That seems like a long time ago, now."

She thought about this before she went on. "I want to tell you something. Most of us spend our lives searching, hoping to find something that will fulfill us. But it isn't what we find in this life that matters, Charlie; it is being found that defines us. I was found by Paul. Do you see?"

"I see," he said, and though what she had told him left him suddenly feeling almost hopeless, he rose up against that feeling. "But I don't want to see," he told her. "You've been found by me now, too. And I'm right here, wanting you, while Paul is in California not wanting you."

"It's not clear to me," she said with some exasperation. "I was always a person who knew what I wanted."

"Me, too," he said. "Things got complicated. For both of us, and maybe the best things we end up doing in life are things we were never certain of."

She asked him if he really believed this.

"Yes, I think I do," he told her. "And here we are. I mean, we were here for each other, right? That has to count for something. We don't know why we were brought together this way. But maybe someday we'll know, and it will all make perfect sense, if we trust what we feel."

She thought for a moment then said, "I don't know, Charlie."

For a long time they sat together in silence, looking up at the sky. Finally he took her hand and said, "Come with me."

They walked hand in hand back to the baggage car, and sat together at the piano. "I'm going to teach you a song," he told her. "I'll hum the notes for you, and you can help me find the right keys."

She agreed. At first he was self-conscious, but soon he found his voice, and after they had the notes down, he taught her the words. It was the song "One" by the Irish band U2. Before long they were singing the refrain together—"One love, one life. We get to carry each other. Carry each other."

"It's a beautiful song," Sally said.

"*Rolling Stone* magazine voted it the best rock love song of all time," he told her, and after she responded with a puzzled expression, he said, "Never mind." He was looking straight into her eyes when he took her hands in his.

"I'm getting off the train in the morning," he said softly. "I want you and Scarlet to come with me."

She didn't oppose him as he thought she might. Her smile was her assent. And then she nodded as well. He took her in his arms and while they embraced she spoke to him. "I just need you to tell me something, Charlie. Tell me that I am wrong about this one thing that I have made myself believe. We can never be sure about these things anyway, but I have had this belief that in the end, when we are old and no longer driven by the fears and desires of our youth, after our hormones have stilled inside us, what will bring us the peace that we all long for is being able to say honestly that we stayed in love with that person we pledged ourselves to."

She paused for a moment. "That we loved that person with all our heart and mind and soul. That life was not about what we wanted, but what we freely gave to that other person. To love, more than to be loved. To understand more than to be understood. Tell me I'm wrong, Charlie, and I will get off this train with you in the morning. And we'll see if we were meant to be together after all."

Charlie's head was bowed when she finished. Slowly, he raised his eyes to look at her. "I'll tell you in the morning," he said.

TWENTY-SIX

*H*e had no memory of walking back to the sleeper car with Sally that night. Maybe he kept his eyes closed as she led the way. Or maybe they held on to each other as they walked through the rocking cars, less like lovers and more like survivors returning from some catastrophe, walking away from a bridge that had collapsed behind them just after they crossed it.

Charlie lay in his bunk for a while with his eyes opened and a fat silver moon sailing across the window before she called his name softly.

"Yes," he called back.

He heard her move in the bed above him, and then her hand hung down and he took hold of it.

"Maybe you should come with us to California," she said.

She leaned over the bunk so he could see her face and her hair spilling through the lambent light of the moon. "Ride with us the rest of the way, and we'll decide what to do when we get there," she said. "Does that make sense?"

This time he sat up so he could take her face in his hands. He kissed her gently, looking deeply into her eyes and letting the motion of the train carry him away with her, so that he was already standing next to her beside the tracks, the child in his arms, in the first light of a new day, in the beginning of a new life that he could make into whatever dream he chose.

He hadn't really slept at all. The faint knock on the door did not surprise him; he seemed to be waiting for it.

It was Maurice. "If you are getting off, it is time, monsieur," was all he said.

Charlie had slept in all his clothes. He stood up, and when he looked at Sally he saw that she had fallen asleep with the telegram in her hand. He knew then that he had to let her go.

He glanced at her one last time, and touched Scarlet's hand before he left the room.

Maurice was hurrying up the corridor. "Two minutes," he said.

"Two minutes," Charlie heard himself repeating.

"So monsieur, you are letting her go. This means that you have become an honorable man."

"I don't know about that," Charlie said quite miserably.

"You don't have to know, monsieur," Maurice countered. "But it is true. And we need every honorable man we can find in this world."

By the time they reached the caboose, the train had slowed to a stop. "So then," Maurice said, shaking Charlie's hand, "Godspeed. I am grateful to have known you in my life."

The old man went back inside. Charlie was about to climb down from the caboose when he saw something shining in the morning light. He bent down, and lying there in the snow on the rear deck were the drumming soldier's metal dog tags that he had thrown to Charlie from the caboose of the eastbound train. Charlie picked them up and read the name stamped into the metal in block letters. Charles Andrews.

He stood up and held the dog tags into the light and read the name again. "My father," he said to himself, and he was filled with wonder.

It took him a moment to remember that he was supposed to get off the train. He jumped down into the snow and began running beside the train, passing each car until he was finally even with the room where Sally stood with Scarlet. Their faces were pressed to the window. The train was moving faster now, and Charlie had to run to keep up. He said the first thing that came into his heart. "I'll always be looking for you."

"You'll find me one day, Charlie," Sally said.

"Are you sure?" he asked her.

"One day, yes," she said.

"When we've grown old?" he asked.

"Oh, Charlie," she said, "we're much too young to ever grow old."

The train was making such noise that Charlie didn't quite hear this. "What?" he called to her.

"What?" she called back. But it was lost, and all she and the child could do was wave to him as he fell behind. They watched him waving back to them as the space between them grew. At one point, when they were separated by maybe fifty yards, he started running, sprinting as fast as he could to close the distance, and for a little while, he was closing the distance and it seemed like he would catch up to them again, but then the train gained speed on him and they began waving to each other once more.

Charlie watched until the last car disappeared. And when he turned to walk away, up ahead of him in the slanting light of dawn, he saw the little station where Johnny had hopped off the train. There it was, exactly as it had been before, and standing beside it was the lit up Christmas tree with its gold star exactly as it was.

Charlie stood there a moment, as the gold star came into focus. Once he turned back to look in the direction of the train, as if to get his bearings in reality, but only for a moment before he accepted the fact that the train was gone and Sally and the child were gone, and that they had not been real after all. He was walking toward the station as he made his peace with this. It had all been only a dream. He had arrived here in the hands of Fate, or God, for some purpose he might never comprehend, and though it left him feeling unsatisfied, he would have to accept it. Sally was not real. She was, he would tell himself, nothing more than an angel in a fever dream. A fever that had swallowed him after months of punishing stress at work. That was it, he decided. And yet, despite himself, he turned back once more to see if the train was still visible. There was nothing. No trace of sound or sight to lead anyone to believe there had ever been a train there moving out into the distance.

He had walked just a little way when he stopped to put his father's dog tags around his neck. As he did this he saw the St. Christopher medal Sally had given him. He had forgotten all about it, but as he held it in his hand and turned it in the light he heard himself saying, "This is real! This really happened."

In the next instant, he was running to the station as fast as he could go. He burst through the door to discover that he was staring at a big digital clock on the wall with red numbers. It was a room filled with people on cell phones. Here beside him was a teenage girl plugged into her iPod. And over there, across the room, were a handful of well-dressed people drinking steaming cups of coffee as they stared up at CNN on a flat-screen TV mounted to the wall.

Charlie felt himself drifting toward the lighted screen. He got close enough to hear the broadcaster saying something about a blizzard that had brought record snowfalls to the northeastern part of the United States.

He rushed to the clerk at the counter and said loudly enough for the room to fall silent around him, "I need to get to California!"

This was enough to unnerve the clerk, who eyed him suspiciously.

"No, please, listen," Charlie said, this time pleading with a soft voice. "I have to get to California."

The clerk explained that he could take a train to Vancouver and from there he could make connections with Amtrak. "Okay," he said. "When is the next train?"

"The day after tomorrow," she informed him.

"Day after tomorrow!" he cried out. And then he caught himself and said just above a whisper, "Oh no, you don't understand. I really have to get to California right away, miss."

At that moment the clerk's cell phone began to ring, a jaunty rendition of the Rolling Stones "Satisfaction."

"Excuse me," she said.

"Yes, I'm sorry, of course," he said. He began to hang his head until he remembered his own cell phone. He reached into one pocket for it, and when it wasn't there he began going through all his pockets, working both hands frantically. Finally he found it, but it was as cold as ice and wouldn't start up. He was slapping it against his leg to try to get it going as a panic began to rise slowly through him. Then the clerk said, "You can fly from Edmonton."

He snapped to attention at the sound of her voice, but before he could ask her his next question, which was, "How can I get there?" someone called to him from across the room. When he turned, he saw Johnny standing there, holding the door open. "I got a ride for you, kid," he said.

Charlie was stunned, but he hurried towards him and out the opened door as Johnny tipped his hat to him with a flourish. "Have you got a car?" Charlie asked him frantically.

"No, not exactly," Johnny replied. He led the way around the side of the station, then stopped in front of a bright red snowmobile whose driver, an Eskimo in a Davey Crockett coonskin cap, was revving the engine. Charlie jumped on the back without deliberation and as they pulled away, Johnny called after them, "Merry Christmas, Charlie!"

Charlie didn't hear this. For the next half hour, he hung on to the Eskimo as they flew across the frozen countryside.

TWENTY-SEVEN

*H*e traveled through Christmas Eve, and Christmas morning he jumped from the taxi in front of the U.S. Army Clinic in BoisVert, California. "Wait, please!" he shouted to the driver, then ran to the double glass doors, passing a half dozen elderly men in wheelchairs who were talking about the Los Angeles Lakers. The doors were locked. Charlie shook them gently at first, not wanting to annoy anyone. He was aware of the old men talking. One fellow, obviously hard of hearing, shouted, "They might be back in first place, but it depends on what happened to San Antonio."

"I already told you, San Antonio's game in Chicago was cancelled because of a snowstorm," another shouted back at him.

"How do I get in here?" Charlie said, interrupting them.

"Go around to the side, it's always unlocked," one of the men said.

The door he entered opened onto a narrow corridor that seemed as long as a football field. Both sides were lined with men in wheelchairs, most of them old men with their heads bowed, fast asleep, but some of them were younger than Charlie, missing arms and legs. Something cold blew through Charlie's chest and left him feeling dull and hollow as he began moving past them, looking for a nurse or doctor. He thought of the old men having come to this place on trains like the one he'd just been on when they were still boys, and growing old here, day by day, as time passed remorselessly. And the young men who would grow old as he would in the days ahead, none of them ever having the chance he'd had to live in the real world. He began speaking the same three sentences over and over as he walked along: "I'm looking for someone named Sally. She married a soldier named Paul. I don't know his last name." None of the men looked up at him or acknowledged him in any way. He kept looking at their faces and then out ahead of him for someone in charge, and the corridor seemed to be growing longer as he marched on and grew more and more desperate. Yesterday, he thought. Yesterday, I was . . . he closed his eyes and felt Sally in his arms standing in the baggage car. He saw Maurice's red moustache. Snow blowing past the windows. He smelled the coal smoke from the locomotive. Yesterday was . . . a dream.

Finally he was showing the veterans the St. Christopher medallion and saying, "I don't know if she was real or just a dream, but this is real, isn't it? You can see it, can't you?" He was almost at the end of the corridor when one of the men looked up at him. "What's your name, fella?" he said.

"I'm Charlie Andrews."

"I don't know you," he said, "but I know a vet named Paul Briggs. He's married to a gal named Sally."

Charlie dropped down to his knees in front of the man. "Can you tell me how to find them?"

It was the last thing that the man said to him— "I know she's not well."—that played over and over inside Charlie's head as he watched the little town's buildings pass by from the back seat of the cab. A gas station, a hardware store, a bank made of bricks that were pink in the light. When they stopped at an intersection, he watched a young couple walking hand in hand up the sidewalk. And as the boy pulled his girl close, Charlie felt his chest tighten. Then he became aware of a voice on the car radio talking ominously about new unemployment figures. "Turn it off," he snapped at the driver. "Turn off the radio."

He watched the driver's hand reach to the dashboard and in the next moment he was ordering him to go faster, faster, while it was all gathering like a storm inside Charlie, the shame he had felt over losing his father's money, the blinding despair he had felt on the window ledge of the Waldorf, the through-the-looking-glass world of the troop train that had set his head spinning, the redemption he experienced when he let Sally go, and now the old overwhelming Wall Street determination to get her back.

He was out the door of the taxi before it had even stopped, charging up a wheelchair ramp that led to the front door where he stood pounding with one fist, and then with both. He was breathless when the door swung open. An elderly man in a wheelchair was on the other side. "Where's Sally?" Charlie cried to him. "Where is she?" Before the man could answer, Charlie turned slightly and saw a flash of sunlight across a lake. He heard loons calling out across the wide sheet of water, and waves washing rhythmically onto the shore. For a moment he closed his eyes and felt like he could fall asleep and drift away.

"Who are you?" he heard the man saying.

"Who am I? I'm Charlie. I need to know something. Who are you?" He stopped suddenly, and for the second time in the last half hour, he dropped to his knees.

The elderly man in a plaid wool shirt was handsome, with hands that were tanned from the sun. He wore a gold cross on a chain around his neck and answered in a quiet voice. "My name's Paul Briggs. Somebody called me from the VA clinic and told me about you."

Charlie looked up into the man's eyes, which were soft and gray.

He took hold of his shoulders and said, "Is she an angel? Is Sally an angel?"

At first the man looked like he wasn't going to answer Charlie's question. But then he said proudly, "She's my angel, yes."

He had a blanket draped over his legs, but under his shoes Charlie could see iron braces like the ones Scarlet had worn.

Charlie rose slowly to his feet and felt the tension begin to drain from him, though the man's answer had told him nothing. Suddenly he put out his hand for Charlie to shake. "When they called me from the clinic and told me your name, it explained the phone calls I've been getting."

"What do you mean?" Charlie asked him.

"I don't know how your father's cell phone got into my Sally's coat pocket. But he called here. I was going to have my daughter mail this to him," he said, as he took the cell phone from his lap.

"Scarlet?" Charlie said.

"You know my daughter, too?"

"It's a long story," Charlie said.

"Well, come in," Paul said as he handed Charlie his father's phone. "Scarlet will be by this morning. She comes by every morning. I have three daughters actually, and five grandchildren." He was already pointing to the mantle above a whitewashed brick fireplace where there was a row of photographs in frames. The only one that Charlie was interested in was the one of Sally standing with a handsome young soldier in uniform. He walked slowly to the fireplace and took it in his hands. "Your wedding day," Charlie said.

"Sixty-four years ago today," Paul said. "We were married at two o'clock in the afternoon in a rainstorm. I almost didn't get to marry her. Truth is, she was on a train across the country on her way here, when I sent her a telegram telling her not to come. I'd been wounded in the last week of the war and I didn't want her to have to spend her life pushing around a cripple. She always told me that she might have listened to me if it weren't for this fellow on the train, a farmer from Alberta, Canada, who talked her into coming."

Charlie felt his heart pounding. And then the world began to whirl around him and he dropped down in the nearest chair.

"Are you okay?" Paul asked him.

"Maybe I should have a glass of water," he replied.

"Sure, not a problem," Paul said.

Charlie heard the motor on the wheelchair whirring in the next room and as he stared at Sally's face in the photograph, he kept running his left hand over the arm of the chair and telling himself that this was real, that he was in California now and that California was as real as the chair he was sitting in. To make sure that his mind was working, he recalled the year he had graduated from college, 1999. And then when he finished business school at Harvard in 2002. Then Paul returned with his glass of water.

"The hospice people are with her now," he said, gesturing to the carpeted hallway that ran away from them.

"I'm sorry," Charlie said.

Paul nodded. "Whenever I think about living without Sally, I can't really get a picture of what my life will be like. We've had a long run together, a wonderful life, but when you reach the end, you always want more time."

For a moment the man drifted away on his own thoughts. Charlie watched as he folded and unfolded his hands, and turned his wedding ring on his finger. Finally he said, "And you knew Sally from the VA clinic, is that it?"

It was so much easier for Charlie to just agree, rather than try to explain how he had found his way here. And so he did.

TWENTY-EIGHT

*P*aul showed Charlie around the little house that was filled with knickknacks, tiny plaster sculptures, souvenirs, and figurines he couldn't identify. There were plastic curtains at the window in the kitchen, and plastic flowers on the dining room table. It was exactly the kind of place Charlie would have made fun of most of his life, and considered it a fate worse than death were he made to live there. Paul was most proud of his collection of framed Elvis photographs, taken at various venues. "We saw him in concert fifteen times," he announced with pleasure. "This one is Sally's favorite over here." And there she was, in her forties perhaps, being kissed on the cheek by Elvis in his powder blue cape. "That was the last concert he did in Vegas," Paul said.

Charlie nodded his head thoughtfully. He heard loons calling across the lake once again, and felt his eyes closing with exhaustion. Suddenly all he wanted was to lie down and sleep for a while.

Just then two hospice women came into the room. Charlie stood alone at the kitchen sink while Paul accompanied them to the front door. When he returned, the two men looked at each other for a moment. Then Paul spoke.

"Why don't you come say hello to my wife," he said. "Or goodbye."

"May I?" Charlie asked.

"Yes, of course," Paul told him.

Charlie followed him down the hall to an open door at the end. Even before he stepped inside, he saw her beautiful white hair spread across the pillow. Her bed had been pushed up to a window so she could look out at the lake to a dock where a small sailboat was tied. "Stars drowning in the lake," Charlie said to himself as he walked silently to the bed.

He knelt down next to her, beside a small table where there was a vase with more plastic flowers and a framed black and white photograph of Sally's wedding day, with Scarlet standing beside her in her wonderful dress. As he leaned closer to study the faces in the picture, he felt her breath on his skin. It was the only thing that made him feel real, and made her real to him. As real as they had both been on the train. As he looked at her, she raised one hand and brushed her hair from her face the way she had before she spoke to him the first time outside his room in the sleeper car. Already she inhabited his memory so vividly that he seemed to remember nothing else from his past. It was as if his past belonged to her completely.

Paul left them alone together, but Charlie didn't stay long. Trying to reconcile the image of Sally in the picture with the person laying on the bed was the most difficult thing he'd ever done in his life. She never opened her eyes. The shallow cadence of her breathing never varied. He thought of kissing her goodbye, but instead he simply touched her forehead, then turned and walked to the doorway, where he looked back once more before stepping out into the hall. He could see Paul at the far end, in the living room, his wheelchair pushed to a table.

Charlie put his hand in his coat pocket as he began walking away from the bedroom, felt his iPhone, took it out, and saw its lighted screen. He turned back and walked to Sally once more.

She hadn't moved or changed her expression, but something about her seemed different to him now. A moment passed, then he held the phone in his palm, looking down at its lighted dial. He opened the file that contained his music and scrolled down the list of songs until he found the one by U2 that he wanted. As soon as it began, he felt like he was back on the train with Sally, working out the chords on the piano in the baggage car.

He sat on the bed and took her hand. He closed his eyes and he was there again with her. He could even feel the rocking of the train. Tears began rolling down his cheeks. And then he felt her squeeze his hand. When he opened his eyes she was looking right at him with that same old smile, as serene and comforting as the moon. In that moment they seemed to have traveled a great distance together since he first saw her, across oceans of time, through the deep silence of light and shadow. "This song," he said softly, "do you remember?"

She didn't answer, but he saw the look of recognition in her eyes. And then while he was watching, her smile vanished and an uneasiness swept across her face. He thought of calling for her husband, but she was already speaking to him with an urgency in her voice. "You are going to wonder in the end if what you remember was real. All you'll have are your memories, but they won't seem real anymore. You have to believe me, they are. They are real."

Charlie waited, but there was nothing more. Finally he slipped the St. Christopher necklace over her head. When he gently touched her hand, she whispered, "All those things you believed when you were little were real, too. We forget them all our lives, but at the end we remember them again. You know this now."

He nodded.

"Don't waste a day," she whispered.

There were many things he still couldn't understand, but this made sense to him. "I won't," he told her.

TWENTY-NINE

*H*e turned away and saw Paul waiting at the threshold. He walked toward him, wanting to tell him something that would make this easier for him, easier for both of them. But he was too sad to say anything, and it was Paul who spoke first. "She rode a train across the country to marry me sixty-four years ago today," he said with a low, soft voice. "She always spoke about two people on the train with her. One was the young farmer from Canada. I don't know his name or whatever happened to him. But the other was a nurse. Her name was Martha Kelly. She was from Brooklyn, and she returned there after the war and started a home of some kind for veterans. We used to get a card from her every Christmas. She would be in her eighties by now, like us, so maybe she's gone. I called there the other day and there was no answer."

Charlie heard him but wasn't really listening. The branches of a tree were tossing in the wind outside the window across from the bed, and he watched the shifting patterns of sunlight and shadow on the pale yellow quilt that covered Sally, trying to discern if she was still breathing. "Yes, I remember there was a nurse on the train," he said, without moving his eyes from the bed.

"I don't understand," he heard Paul say. "What do you mean—you remember?"

The two men looked at each other, while Charlie tried to understand what he was asking. "I'm sorry," Charlie said, "I wasn't listening."

Paul began to move down the hallway, speaking to Charlie while he followed behind. "I was telling you about a nurse in Brooklyn," he said. "She was on the train with Sally and you said, 'I remember.'"

Charlie said, "What I meant was, Sally told me about her. But if you have an address or a phone number, I could look her up for you when I get back to New York."

"I have it here," Paul said.

Charlie stayed in the living room while Paul went through some drawers in the next room. He looked around again at the photographs and their simple possessions gathered over time. They marked the arc of a modest life and were intended, he knew, to show that even a plain and ordinary story has beautiful moments of being that are worth remembering across the years.

Paul returned soon with the address and telephone number.

"If she's still there, what do you want me to say to her?" Charlie asked.

"Well, I'm not sure she's even still alive, like I said," Paul answered. "But I asked your father—"

Charlie interrupted. "My father?"

"Yes, when he called here looking for his phone and he said that he was in New York, I asked him if he could help me find my granddaughter. When she first moved to New York, we told her about the nurse in Brooklyn, in case she ever needed any help. My wife and I were both worried from the beginning." He paused for a moment, then added, "I was going to send her a plane ticket to come see her grandmother, even though she's afraid to fly."

Charlie had let his eyes wander again, this time to a single plastic rose set in a milk glass vase on a windowsill. Now he turned sharply and faced the man. "What did you say?" he asked.

Paul looked at Charlie as if he were trying to measure him in some way. "My granddaughter is afraid to fly," he said with a new sadness in his voice.

Charlie felt a chill, like a spark, cross the back of his neck. Both his hands began to tremble and when he spoke next, the sound of his own voice surprised him. "What's your granddaughter's name?" he asked. Then when Paul answered that her name was Sally and that she had been named after his wife, all Charlie could think about was how much time it was going to take for him to get from this little house to an airport, and then how he was going to sit in a plane for all those hours until he landed in New York City. He looked out the window and saw the taxi was still there, waiting for him. He was already moving in the direction of the door when he asked Paul to please tell him what he wanted to say to this granddaughter should he find her.

"A year ago, she was engaged to this really nice young man, but after he was killed in Iraq, I'm afraid we lost her."

"What do you mean, you lost her?" Charlie pressed.

"Growing up, she and her grandmother were always very close, and after Tony was killed, she began telling people her grandmother's story, you know, the story about how she rode a train across the country to marry me on Christmas day. We spoke with her by phone a few times and you could tell she was just sort of vanishing, the way people do sometimes when they're hurt."

It was becoming clear to Charlie now, and when they were outside, he told Paul that he was going to look for Sally first in Brooklyn at the veterans' home, and if she wasn't there, he was going to search the city for as long as it took. "Until I find her," he said.

Paul thanked him and nodded. Then he got a troubled look in his eyes and said there was something else that he wanted him to know. "I don't want you to think less of my wife when I tell you this," he said. "She's a wonderful woman, she really is. But she's tough, you know? I guess she had to be tough looking after me all these years. Anyway, she's one of those people who believes that when life knocks you down, you have to grab hold of your bootstraps and pull yourself back up and go on marching. Do you know what I mean, Charlie?"

"Yes," he said.

"She didn't really understand when our granddaughter couldn't get going again," he said. "The few times they talked, well, there wasn't much understanding, I'm afraid. That's why I really want them to be together now before it's too late."

Charlie waited a moment, then said that he understood. "There's something I need to tell you," he went on. "It might not make sense to you, and really, I can't quite grasp it myself. But I think your granddaughter was on her way home, on her way here for Christmas. She was on a train, the same train that I was on, but she got off. I think that she was trying to come back, but she couldn't."

"You'll do your best to find her?" Paul asked.

"You have my word," Charlie said. He felt a silence above him, and with it a new sense of all that was possible in the world. He seemed to be coming out of a suspension of time, shaking off that feeling of unreality and numbness that comes when you are deprived of sleep.

Before Charlie got into the cab, Paul thanked him again and then said one last thing. "People say all the time that life is short, but it isn't really, it's long. It's just that it goes by faster than you can ever imagine."

*U*nlike dear Charlie, who slept in the sky that night with the same stars that were drowning in the California lake, and a silver half moon sailing beside him, and a few dozen weary Christmas travelers crossing America together thirty-three thousand feet above the ground on their way to New York City, I was just putting one foot in front of the other, walking the old Flatbush neighborhood of Brooklyn like I had ten thousand times before on my way home from work as a security guard at Madison Square Garden, passing the lit up boxes of light where families were together at that hour of the evening when their lives are covered in a descending stillness, almost like innocence, and when I always feel kind of temporary about myself, a man who never married or had children, a man who got up in the morning, read the paper, packed his lunch, and went to work each day. I never pass those families in their rooms where the lights are burning without thinking about my boyhood and my grandmother in her flower-print dress, and the little row houses in my town that the soldiers had left for the war. Of course they are all lost and gone now—my grandmother, and those houses and the people who filled them with children and enough joy and sorrow to last a lifetime. But when I reach out to them in my memory as I did that Christmas night, crossing through the snow to St. John's Place, I always see them young and strong in the fullness of their time, husbands in crew cuts, wives in lipstick and nylon stockings, their arms around each other, and their eyes bright with passion as if they almost believed that they could go on forever that way, so that at the end of their lives they would have no regrets, they would not have to wish that they had loved each other better when they had the chance.

Charlie's flight would have begun its approach into JFK that night at the time I climbed Clayborne Hill, and as I glanced into the sky, there was one light a little brighter than the stars and moving steadily to the east that could have been the light on the tip of his wing. When I lowered my eyes, I saw a man peering in the windows of the handsome four-story brownstone at the corner of Rush and Pilmore, the soldiers' home, as it was known by the residents of the neighborhood. Over the years I'd spoken many times with the old World War II vets who passed through there, and then with the sad young men back from Vietnam who looked like pirates, with their moustaches and bandanas. Lately there had been a procession of soldiers from Iraq and Afghanistan, who smoked their cigarettes on the granite steps in front at all hours of the night. They looked lost and much too young to have gone so far from home and fought in a war. I had only been inside the building once, three years earlier, to pay my respects, when the dignified and elderly woman who ran the place passed away. All I knew about her was that she had raised twin sons who were once star running backs on the P.S. 334 high school football team, and that she was supposedly worth a lot of money. Beneath a photograph of her in uniform as a young Army nurse from the Second World War, I had signed the condolence book with a gold fountain pen.

From where I stood that night, the man peering in the windows looked a little stooped in the shoulders and unsteady on his feet as he stepped over the snowbanks, moving slowly from window to window. I could have just kept walking and I was tempted, but it was such a cold night, and I thought the man might be a resident at the home who had somehow locked himself out.

As I stepped into the street to cross over to him, I noticed that the light in the foyer, a beautiful chandelier that I often admired as I passed, was off. "Are you lost?" I called out when I reached the sidewalk. I had taken the man by surprise and when he turned to face me, I saw that he was a harmless-looking old fellow with white hair.

"That's the right word," he said, as he took his gloves

off, then held his hand out for me to shake. "I feel lost, alright," he went on. "But if this is Sixteen St. John's Place, then I'm where I've been told to be."

"Who told you to be here?" I asked him.

"It's a long story," he replied. "This man who answered my phone. This man in California. Anyway, here I am, and I keep hearing voices but no one answers the door. He paused, tilted his head, and listened intently. "There," he exclaimed. "Can you hear that?"

I could barely make out the sound of a voice, but I knew at once that it wasn't coming from inside. "I heard something," I told him. "It seems like it's coming from somewhere else."

"Maybe you're right. Where?" he asked.

Before I could answer, we both heard the sound again, and I started walking down the narrow path alongside the building with him close behind. "I lost my phone four days ago," I heard him say. "Somehow it got to California. And like I said, this man asked me if I would look for someone here." Now his voice trailed away as we continued on and some time passed. The sound grew louder and then defined itself as voices grew clearer while we made our way down the long flank of the building, both of us, I suspect, as reluctant as we were curious to know its meaning. When we reached the end of the path, we moved out into the open and walked across a wide parking lot to the source of the sound, which was a two-car garage under a flat metal roof standing in a band of moonlight. I had the flashlight I always took to work, and when I turned it on and held it to one of the small windows on the garage door, I couldn't believe what I was looking at. Inside there were maybe a dozen people huddled together around a space heater that was glowing red. It took both of us to kick the padlocked door off its hinges and when we saw that the people inside had been tied together with rope, we stood in the threshold like dummies too shocked to move.

Soon they were all talking at once and it took some time to sort out what had happened. On Christmas Eve, a young sergeant, an Army explosives expert who had just returned from Afghanistan, had rounded up all the residents of the soldiers' home at gunpoint and herded them into the garage. "He might have been on drugs," one man said.

"I don't think so," a younger man added. "He was just cool, that's all. One smoking, cool dude. He's wired the place to blow to smithereens. He told me he wanted to go out with a bang. I think he would have done it by now, but the girl wouldn't leave. She told him that he was going to have to kill her, too, and I don't think he has it in him."

"What girl?" I heard the old fellow asking.

That's when another man spoke up. He was one of

three people in wheelchairs, and I could see that he was shivering. "She'd been living in a cardboard box on Park Avenue," he said slowly," until she showed up here Christmas Eve."

"She's still in there with him?" I asked.

"No way to know," the younger man said. And the others agreed. They'd been locked in the garage for almost twenty-four hours.

"If he was going to blow the place up, he would have done it by now," someone else called out. "He's bluffing."

"Does anyone here have a cell phone?" I asked.

No one did and the old man told me once again that he had lost his.

"All right," I said. "Everyone stays right here while I find a pay phone and call the police."

I was back on the street in front of the house and had just begun to walk to the park when something made me turn back. I heard the glass shatter, as the old man kicked in one panel on the front door, reached inside to turn the lock, then stepped into the dark foyer, closing the door behind him.

I felt the air rush from my lungs in one burst. Then all the sound in the city seemed to fall away to silence. A taxi was coming to a stop in front of the house, but it was floating noiselessly. And when the young man stepped out onto the sidewalk and threw the taxi door closed, I heard nothing. It was all very strange for the next few minutes, and I felt the way I had as a young man, gunning the accelerator on my first car and throwing it into a tailspin across the ice in the parking lot of the Acme supermarket just to see how it would feel, and then wanting it to stop.

The young man from the cab introduced himself, and I explained as best I could what was happening, then made him promise that he would stay out of harm's way until I called the police and they had arrived. "My father's in there?" he said.

"If your father lost his cell phone and it ended up in California, then the answer is yes," I told him. "And no matter what kind of big shot you've been in your life, don't try to be a hero, okay? Stay right here until I get back."

"Where are you going?" he asked me.

"To call the police," I said, already walking away.

"I have my cell," he said. "But I don't want the girl to get in any trouble."

"What do you mean? You know the girl?"

"I do," he told me. "She was on a train with me to California, but she got off. We sort of lost each other."

"Must be a different girl," I told him. "This one is homeless. She was living in a cardboard box—"

Before I could finish, the chandelier went on and the three of them appeared in the foyer. The soldier, a diminutive young man who looked like a teenager in a gold hooded sweatshirt, gold basketball sneakers, and faded blue jeans that hung low on his narrow hips, stood with his head bowed between a young woman and the old man, who held the boy's arm with one hand, and in the other, the pistol.

Charlie ran across the street and as he drew near, the old man called out to him: "Charlie, Charlie, is that you?"

"It's me, Pop," he said.

"I've been trying to reach you."

"I know, Pop."

"What are you doing here?" the old man asked.

"I'll explain," Charlie said.

And then I watched him take Sally in his arms. There was a moment when I just stood there, watching as he held her, and then when he took his father's hand, I felt like I was in the presence of something I might never completely understand. But it made me feel privileged.

As I crossed the street to join them, it began to snow, big fat flakes swirling down silently from the sky. I heard Sally saying how sorry she was for getting off the train. "We stopped in Stockbridge," she said. "You were sleeping. I thought about seeing my grandmother again, I mean, about her seeing me this way, and I thought about how I had lied to you, and I panicked. Some man helped me to a train back to New York."

"His name was Johnny wasn't it?" Charlie said.

"Yes. Yes, that's right," she said.

"Didn't you trust me?" he asked her.

"I did," she said softly.

"You didn't," Charlie said, "or you would have just told me the truth."

She bowed her head, then raised her eyes to him. "Oh, Charlie," she said. " That was my grandmother's beautiful story. She told it to me the first time when I was just a little girl. Really, Charlie, I don't have a story of my own."

Charlie smiled and looked into her eyes. "You do now," he said. "And your grandmother is waiting for you."

"She's waiting for me?"

He nodded and told her that she had to go home.

"I'm not sure I can face her," she told him again.

"You can," he told her. "I'll come with you. We'll go together. But we're going to have to fly. We don't have any time to waste."

He asked his father if he remembered riding a train across Canada after the war.

"Of course I do," his father said.

"Do you remember a nurse on board in the car with the wounded soldiers?"

"I do. I remember her."

"This is her place."

His father turned and looked back at the house incredulously, as Charlie told him that she had taken care of soldiers here.

"Well, that's something, isn't it," his father said. After a moment he turned to the soldier who stood beside him shivering and shifting his weight from one foot to the other. "Are you doing anything tonight around dinner time?" he asked him.

The boy looked surprised. "No," he said. "Nothing special."

"Alright then," Charlie's father said. "I'll swing by and we'll have a meal somewhere. How's that sound to you, soldier?"

The boy nodded. "Good," he said. "Thanks."

Charlie and Sally took the next plane for the West Coast. They insisted that I go with them to the airport and we all had a little time together in the terminal. There was a moment when I watched the three of them talking together like any family, before I said goodbye and headed back to Brooklyn.

The only thing left to tell you is that Charlie's money troubles were over. In the third drawer on the left of Martha Kelly's mahogany rolltop desk was a manila envelope with his name on it. She had set aside money to repay him a portion of the fortune she made from the stock tips he gave her, in the unlikely event that he should ever find his way to the soldier's home. Inside the envelope was a safe deposit box number and directions to the Duchess Country Savings and Loan near her summer place in South Hampton, where there was more money waiting for Charlie than even he could spend in a lifetime.

The End

ACKNOWLEDGEMENTS

The speech given by the soldier called Chief is taken from what is widely believed to have been a speech by Chief Seattle, patriarch of the Duwamish and Suquamish Indians of Puget Sound.

Special thanks to Via Rail, which allowed me to travel across Canada one winter on the marvelous "le Canadien." And to Fairmont Hotels for giving me a place to stay in Montreal at the beginning and in Vancouver at the end of the journey.

Thanks also to Victoria Pryor, who believed in me and in this book when no one else did. And to Jason Kaufman who pushed me hard to figure out the plot. If I got it wrong in the end, it's my fault entirely, not his.